FOR NIGHTS LIKE THIS ONE:
Stories of Loving Women

FOR NIGHTS LIKE THIS ONE:
Stories of Loving Women

by Becky Birtha

FROG IN THE WELL
PO Box 170052
San Francisco, CA 94117

1983

Library of Congress Cataloging in Publication Data

Birtha, Becky, 1948–
    For nights like this one.

    1. Lesbianism—Fiction. I. Title.
PS3552.I7574F67 1983   813'.54   82-21087
ISBN 0-9603628-4-3 (pbk.)

Printed in the United States of America

Typeset by Ann Flanagan Typography

ACKNOWLEDGEMENTS

The author wishes to express thankfulness for the help provided by members of her writing group: appreciation for the support of Meg Brigantine, Paula De Leon, K Gordon, Susan Roberts, Jean Walat, and Susan Windle, and remembrance of the support of Claudia Scott.

for Becky Davidson
with love
and sincere thanks

TABLE OF CONTENTS

IT WAS OVER THEN

"The trouble with you two," Steve had once said to Christie and me, "is that you think because you're roommates, you're married. You ought to be honest about your feelings and live out the relationship fully, or just quit letting yourselves get hurt by each other."

The day we tripped in Rittenhouse Square Park, I was happy and Christie, as usual, was slowly but steadily freaking out. It was midsummer and unbearably hot. She asked if I remembered where the water fountain was, and I pointed and stood up to accompany her, but she jerked away and said, "I can go by myself, you know." So I sat down and watched her across the park. It was always like that between us. She would ask me for something and then, when I tried to give, she'd reject it, put me down. Yet I was never prepared for the next time, always ended up getting hurt again.

Once, she was rearranging her room. She had asked me to help, but I stood in the doorway not sure what to do. Then she knocked against a lamp and as it plunged toward the floor, I caught it, bumping against her. She was furious—said something then, too, about being able to do things for herself. And I knew afterwards I should've said, "Fuck off, I was only trying to help you. You got a lot of nerve putting me down for that." Only I never said that to her.

That day in the square, she came back crying. About the city, sweltering, airless, all concrete and brick—garbage on the ground, traffic noises and fumes, sad old bums and derelicts. . . . "It's so ugly," she said.

1

And I tried to show her how it wasn't—there were children
playing on the lawn by the stone goat, an ice cream vendor,
someone blowing bubbles. . . "and there's a pony cart giving
people rides around the square."
That was too much. "There is not," she said. But there was.
The pony cart was painted bright. There were four or five
people sitting in the wagon. Two of them had rented it for the
day from a junk dealer on South Street. They were giving rides
for free around and around the edge of the square, because it
was hot, because it was July.
People moved over and made room for Christie and me to
climb in. It was shady under the roof and, once we began to
move, there was a bit of a breeze. The boy who sat across from
us was named Neil. He was tall, with blond hair, and smiled a
lot. He was smiling at us, mostly at Christie. And then he was
talking with us, about himself. He had dropped out of school a
year before; at the beginning of the summer he had hitched
down from Boston where his family lived. "It's really amazing,"
he said, "doing it at last, leaving home."
And Christie said yes and I didn't say anything. Christie told
him she'd left her home in Ohio at the beginning of the summer,
too. She didn't say she was living with me at my parents' house
in the near-suburb, Chestnut Hill. I still wasn't going to say
anything but he asked me. And it was so important to me then
to come across as being together, independent, to be an acceptable kind of person.
"I left home when I was seventeen and I went away to school."
He looked at me a long time before he said, not as a question,
but a statement, "You never really left home."
Then it was over, because the police came to give the pony
wagon a ticket for obstructing traffic. I knew it was no good
any longer, and we jumped down, suddenly back in the stifling
city. The breeze ended and heat rose in waves from the sticky
street. I could see the panic rising in Christie's face, and remembered we were still tripping. I wanted to do something to
keep it good for her. So I said, "Neil, why don't you come with
us?" And he smiled and took a hand of each of us.
We took the subway surface car out to West Philadelphia.
We had to change cars at Thirtieth Street, where the station
was like an underground city. Christie got hung up on the es-

calators; she kept going up the up one and down the down one.
Neil and I followed her at first, but after a little we both got
tired, and leaned against the token kiosk watching her. She
never carried a purse, and she had her green army knapsack
strapped on her back. She kept going up and around and down
again, and soon it began to scare me. She looked like some kind
of zombie doing that, the pack on her back, with her fluffy hair
wild and her blue eyes glazed, not looking at us or at anything.

Neil said, "Can't you stop her?" But I didn't want to try, to
have her hurt me.

When she reached the bottom again, he stopped her with
his hand on her shoulder, and Christie drew back. I knew I
didn't want her to be angry with him, but couldn't think what
to do. I started singing softly, "Take your hands off it, don't you
dare touch it / 'Cause you know it don't belong to you. . . ." Neil
looked at me strangely for a moment, and then at Christie the
same way. But it was over. Suddenly it was all right to catch
the trolley, and we got off at Forty-ninth Street and went to
Steve's place.

Steve was dealing acid that summer. Neil bought a tab and
Christie and I each dropped another half to stay with him. We
sat in the living room, letting the music through us, and watching the colors play across the walls and floor, and laughing a
lot. Christie and I were together for once, and we were both
liking Neil. But it was unbelievably hot. The summer afternoon
turned to a Philadelphia summer night, and we sat on the porch
and watched the lightning bugs come out, and it was still hot.
When the truck came around, Neil bought a water ice for Christie
and one for me. Then we took turns taking icy showers. It didn't
help. The heat began to take over, to be the only quality of the
night.

Finally Christie said she knew what we could do. She took
my hand and dragged me into the back room, shutting the door
against Neil and Steve. We took off our cotton dresses and sat
naked on the smooth linoleum tile. We turned off the light against
the heat. I had one cigarette left, and we shared it. It was very
quiet. There began to be a breeze through the open window.

Neil opened the door unexpectedly. None of us moved. For
a long minute he stood there staring at us as we sat motionless
in our nakedness. "You two aren't. . .no, you couldn't be," he

said. "You are, aren't you." Then he slammed out of the room
and I scrambled up and pulled my dress over my head, running
to catch him.

He was standing at the other side of the living room, his face
hard and ugly. He had a beer bottle by the neck in his clenched
fist, uplifted. "Don't come near me. Fucking Dyke!" He lowered
the bottle then and said, "Take me home." I moved a step closer
across the floor. "Don't touch me. Just get me out of here. Take
me home."

Neil and I took the subway surface car to Thirteenth Street,
sitting on opposite sides of the car. We walked to the downstairs
door of the place where he was crashing; then he swore at me
and I left. I found my way back alone through the swirling shadows and blinking lights and long, dark tunnels to Forty-ninth
Street, back to Christie. It was all right. Steve sat on the bottom
step and Christie was standing on the porch above him, watching
for me. Even in the darkness, her shape was glowing bright, a
rim of color around the edges of her hair. I could see the curves
and lines of her slight body under the thin cotton dress.

BABIES

Lurie awoke with a sense of satisfaction, contentment, completion. A second to register Sabra's face—awake, watching, loving her—and she closed her eyes again, snuggling into the crook of Sabra's arm, trying to recapture the source of that contentment. Then she remembered:

"I dreamed there was some emergency or disaster going on," she began. "And there were all these refugee children and babies. Someone was asking people to take one, to take care of them. And I picked out a baby and tied it on my back, and came home to you. And you didn't mind at all; you liked it. You even started to play with it."

Lurie smiled, remembering the fat little creature with the wisps of shining black hair and wide, wondering eyes—bringing it home to Sabra like the best surprise of all. Then she let go, opened her eyes to Sabra's reaction—the furrowed brow, mouth drawn tight. Sabra, Lurie remembered, fully awake now, did not like babies. Didn't share that weakness that would draw Lurie's gaze after a toddler on the street, or cause her to stare hungrily for minutes at an infant on a subway.

She knew Sabra was already interpreting her dream. "Never mind, Sabra," she said. "It was only a dream. I can't help what I dream." She tried to joke. "I haven't got a baby in my backpack."

"I know." Sabra's face, her voice, were gentle again. But the uneasiness which Lurie's dream had caused lingered.

Lurie remembered the first time they had talked about children, long ago in their first months together. It had been winter then, too, and they were walking in town at night, idly window-shopping. The streets were deserted and they walked arm in arm. Lurie had been caught by the display in a children's clothing shop, and had stared wistfully into the window, pointing things out while Sabra stood silently behind her. "That's the kind of stuff I'd like to get for my little girl. Those hooded sweaters, and corduroy jumpers like those."

"Your little girl?" Sabra had asked incredulously.

And Lurie had laughed. "No, Sabra, I don't have a little girl I've been hiding from you. I mean some day—when I do."

They'd walked on, but Lurie had realized after a block or two that Sabra was still silent, and had not taken her arm again. "What are you thinking, Sabra?" she'd asked.

"I'm thinking about what you said. About a little girl. I don't know what you mean. I thought you were serious about us staying together."

Lurie had been startled. It had not occurred to her that those two plans for her future might be mutually exclusive. "I *am* serious about staying together, but . . . well, I guess I've always wanted to have children. And I hadn't thought about how this might make a difference. Haven't you ever wanted to have children?"

"No," Sabra said, "I never have. In fact, I've always wanted to *not* have children. I know it's not the same for you, but I've been gay all my life, and I want to be for the rest of my life, and it does make a difference about things like that. I've always felt like kids were a kind of heterosexual problem, one more way women are oppressed by men. And I've always felt good that I'd be free from that."

Lurie had been thoroughly shaken. Now that she had finally found the one person she felt she could love, that person was completely opposed to her most important dream. As they had talked on for hours, it became clear that Sabra felt just as threatened, just as shaken by this new question between them, as she. In the end, they had left it open—Lurie reluctantly accepting the possibility that she might never have a child, and Sabra, equally reluctantly, accepting that someday they might consider it.

In the beginning, Lurie would sometimes bring it up—point out something she noticed about a child on the street, or comment on a book or film in which an issue of child-rearing was raised. She had hoped that perhaps, in time, Sabra's views might change, that she might be able to interest Sabra in children. But Sabra seemed to value very highly a life-style in which children had no place, and Lurie realized that the subject always created tension and bad feelings between them. After a few months, she had stopped mentioning the matter, and tried to be careful not to let it show that she still wanted a child.

Now years had passed, in which Lurie's and Sabra's love for each other had deepened and expanded, and in which nothing seemed to be missing. Years when there was plenty of time to be together—to go to films and concerts, to take weekend trips to the seashore, to read aloud together. Time to be apart—for Sabra to practice her music, for Lurie to take evening courses at the local college. Time to make daydreams and plans about writing a book together, moving to the country someday, buying land. They were years in which the fun they had together nearly put out of Lurie's head the images she had held since childhood of her future adult life—full of babies and children and family. Nearly, but not completely. There were still times when she thought about children, about whether she herself would ever have a child.

The morning she related her dream was the first time in three years that Lurie had openly brought up the subject of babies. But once she had, the topic seemed to be open between them again. Lurie would find herself now, often, indulging in thoughts about children, or whimsical fantasies. Like partheno-genesis. She, Lurie, would be the one to carry the child in her body, but the baby would be a biological re-creation of Sabra. Lurie imagined a child who would look exactly as Sabra had in those old snapshots that folded out in accordion pleats from the yellow paper folders. A thin little girl in shorts, with pale brown hair in two braids, bangs across her eyes. Lurie would tie plaid ribbons on the ends of the braids. She would make all the child's clothing herself—long white nightgowns with lace at the neck and sleeves, starchy ruffled pinafores. She pictured the little girl walking into the room where Lurie sat stitching the last hem of a lacey pink dress. And the child taking one look and saying, "I'm not gonna wear that!" Sabra all over again. And Lurie laughed out loud at the prospect. Then Sabra had to

know what she was laughing at, and Lurie didn't want to tell
her, which made it seem bad, as if she'd been laughing at Sabra.
So she did tell her. And, amazingly, Sabra laughed, too.
Sometimes Lurie dreamed of a child who would be both of
theirs. Wondered what a cross between the two of them would
look like. Brown or white? Large-boned or small? Black, frothy
hair or pale, straight hair? She pictured a golden child. Golden
skin and soft, fluffy golden hair. She had seen such children
and wanted every one. But then, didn't she want every child
she saw?
Sometimes, now, they talked about it. Parthenogenesis was
not a real possibility, so Lurie talked of artificial insemination.
Sabra would counter every argument, half-serious, half-teasing.
"The baby would still be some man's. And it might be a boy.
And anyway," Sabra said, wrinkling up her nose in a way that
always made Lurie laugh, "who'd want to be pregnant?" When
Lurie said she wouldn't mind being pregnant, Sabra said she
knew some people who thought it was obscene and disgusting.
"How do you know," she continued, laughing, "I wouldn't be
embarrassed to be seen in public with you?"
At times, Sabra would stop teasing and arguing both, and
talk about it seriously. "I wish you could understand," she said
one afternoon, "why I want not to have a child. I think you think
the only reasons are selfish ones, for me. It's true the things I
do with my time are important to me, like my music and my job
and friends—things there might not be time for with a kid. But
it's more than that. It's that I believe women in general should
be able to care about themselves and their own interests, not
always somebody else first. And as a woman, I really value
freedom and independence."
Lurie began to smile, and Sabra immediately caught the meaning behind the smile. "I know," she said. "I'm not so independent and free any more since you came along. But that's another
reason: us. The way we live together and are happy together.
I want it to always be like that. I want to be able to buy a piece
of land, or write our book, or whatever else we want to do. I
don't want everything to change. And I know it would."
"You're right," Lurie conceded. "Of course it would. But
things always change anyway, and how do we know they wouldn't
change for the better?"

Sabra shook her head. "I just don't believe it. I've been around the gay community for a long time, and I've seen what it's like for women who have children—bringing little kids to meetings, or not showing up because they can't get child care. I've heard about women having fights or breaking up with their lovers over the way they're raising the kids. I've seen how women with kids get alienated from the rest of the community. Not just gay women—all women. Like my mother, or your mother. They gave up everything they could have been, their whole identity, just to be mothers, housewives. I wouldn't want that to happen to you—even if you. . . weren't with me. I want you to be able to finish school and be a social worker or anything you want. You know, besides all the other stuff, I think one of the main reasons I don't want us to have a kid is you."

Lurie was quiet for a long time after that. "Sabra," she finally said, "sometimes I think you care about me even more than I care about myself."

Other times, when they talked, Sabra would grow sad and blame herself. "Maybe I'm all wrong," she would say, "acting as if I know more about what's good for you than you do yourself. If you weren't with me, you would probably have a child by now, and it would probably work out fine."

"I'd rather be with you."

"But if you weren't, wouldn't you have figured out some way to get pregnant, and done it?"

"In fact," Lurie told her, "I wouldn't have. I decided, even before I met you that I didn't want to get pregnant with a child I would have to raise by myself. It didn't seem right, bringing a new child into the world to a less than perfect situation. If I wasn't with you, being alone would have kept me from getting pregnant like it did all those years."

"But," Sabra said, "you still did think about having a child. You must have been counting a whole lot on meeting a man you could do that with."

"Well, no," Lurie answered. "I'd pretty much given up on them, too, even before I met you. I was thinking about being a single parent, by adoption."

She had thought about adoption far more seriously than Sabra knew. In the years before she had met Sabra, she had taken books about it from the library and talked with pediatric social workers. She had even been on the mailing lists of several agencies who sent appealing pictures of wistful little faces starved for love. She knew there were some children whom agencies felt it almost impossible to place. Children who were black or mixed in race, or retarded, emotionally disturbed or physically handicapped. Those who were over three, or over six. Or children who were all of these things. Even in the years before she was with Sabra, she had wondered whether the desire to have a child, or the love she felt she could offer one was great enough to overcome obstacles like those. She had tried to imagine a child she might adopt—not an innocent baby, but a child already full of the hurt and rejection, the mistrust and resentment that six or seven years in foster homes and institutions could cause. Lurie wondered, even then, if it would be worth it, to try to take that on by herself.

Now, being with Sabra, she couldn't overlook another fact she knew about adoption agencies. That there were some adults with whom they would not consider placing even such "impossible" children. And that among these adults were lesbians. Even if Sabra agreed to adopt a child, Lurie realized it would be difficult. Probably it would mean lying and deception. Perhaps living apart, denying their lesbianism. Could their relationship survive that? And what if Sabra would never agree to try to have a child? That brought her to the real question. Did she, Lurie, want one, any child, enough to do it by herself, enough to leave Sabra in order to do it? To leave the one person she had found who she knew loved her, for a child she could not be certain of getting, or whose love she could not be certain of, either? She felt the question closing in on her, felt pushed to make some decision, to reach some resolution. She was thirty-two.

On the Saturday morning before Christmas, when she and Sabra were in town doing the last of their shopping, Lurie noticed a woman who looked familiar standing near them at a stationery counter. She stared at the woman a second or two, then recognized her—an old friend from school that she hadn't seen in six years. Lurie introduced her to Sabra who waited patiently while the other two tried to catch each other up on the events of the past few years. Lurie was brief—she was unable to disclose the changes in her life that really mattered. In turn, the friend told of her marriage, ending by calling a little girl from a few feet away and introducing her as her daughter.

"Your daughter?" Lurie stared at the child of four or five in the fur-trimmed cape and hood, and then again at her friend who was, she remembered, the same age as she.

As if she could read Lurie's thoughts, the woman asked, "You have any children yet?"

Lurie shook her head. "No, not . . . no."

After another minute or two they parted, to continue with their shopping. Lurie was lost in her own thoughts as they wandered through the rest of the store and out into the street, completely forgetting their intended purchase. Sabra was silent, too, and it was some time before Lurie was startled by Sabra's asking, "Are you ready to go home, or what?"

Lurie nodded, and as they turned the corner, Sabra shoved her free hand into her pocket. Once they were home, Sabra managed to be always in a different room from Lurie, the whole afternoon. Lurie could read Sabra's mood in the way she sat as they lingered at the table after dinner—hunched up with her arms folded in on herself, not sitting back, relaxed and open as she usually did. When Sabra asked what she wanted to do that evening, Lurie said she had thought they might visit friends. Seconds later, Sabra abruptly walked out of the kitchen while Lurie was still doing the dishes. Lurie found her later curled up under the afghan on the bed, crying.

She sat on the bed and put her arms around Sabra, afghan and all, and asked what was wrong.

"Nothing."

"Yes there is. Tell me what it is."

"No, there isn't. If you want to go visit people tonight, why don't you go ahead?" Yet Lurie knew Sabra was not crying about visiting friends.

"Tell me, Sabra." She began to plant kisses, little quiet ones, against the back of Sabra's neck and in her hair. "Please tell me." More kisses, until Sabra finally turned and let it spill.

"I just feel like you don't love me as much as you used to. It feels like I'm not enough for you, that you keep wanting some-body else, somebody more."

"That's not true. You know I only want you. There isn't any-body else. . . ."

"I don't mean another woman," Sabra said. "I mean a baby.
I used to think," she went on, "that it was just left over from
when you were alone, and that you wanted a kid because you
just needed somebody to love. And after we'd been together
awhile, you did stop talking about it and I thought maybe your
ideas were changing, and you were appreciating how nice our
life is with just us. But now, ever since we brought it up again,
you want to talk about it all the time, as if it's all you think about.
I've tried to listen to what you say, but I just can't see it that
way. And I've tried to tell you how I feel but it seems like you
don't care. Lurie, you mean so much to me, I don't understand
why it's not the same for you. You have me, and I thought we
were happy. . . ."

"Oh, Sabra. I am happy. You *do* mean a whole lot to me. It's
just that. . ." and she felt Sabra stiffen as she said those last
three words. How could she explain to Sabra what she had
been struggling with in her mind? How could she even suggest
the decision she felt compelled to make, one way or the other?
Yet she had to be honest. "It's just that I've been thinking about
kids a lot these days because I feel like I have to work it out.
Wanting a baby doesn't mean I don't love you or don't want to
be with you. But I can't help wanting a baby. It's just there and
I can't make it go away. Maybe I'll always want one."

She waited, still holding Sabra, afraid of what Sabra's response might be. But Sabra only said, "Can't I be your baby?"

And Lurie said, "You are. You are my baby." And she held
her and rocked her very gently as she would have rocked the
child she had always wanted to love.

During the Christmas holidays, Lurie went to spend a day at
her mother's house. She had been meaning, for a long time, to
go through a closet full of odds and ends left over from her childhood and adolescence. She meant to take what she still wanted
to her own home with Sabra, and to throw the rest out.

She poured through old copybooks and social studies papers,
boxes of costume jewelry, and picture post cards from nearly
forgotten friends. Her mother came in to join her under the pre-
text of cleaning out a cedar chest full of old clothing which
was in the same room. They talked casually about people on the
block, about the latest news from relatives.

When Lurie pulled out a small trunk and opened it to find it full of her childhood dolls, her mother came over to join her. Together, they went slowly through its contents. There were a dozen dolls, one from every Christmas until Lurie was twelve—babies, toddlers, little girls with impish or pouting or smiling faces. Lurie remembered those Christmas mornings, so different from the quietly happy one which had just passed, when she and Sabra had stayed in bed cuddling and talking long into the morning, when there had been no dolls or toys under their Christmas tree. She still remembered the name of every doll. They had been her children, all those years when she was still certain she would have real babies some day.

Each of the dolls had a complete wardrobe. There were little dresses of plaid and checked and printed fabrics, aprons, nightgowns, coats. Lurie turned them over in her hands, touching the tiny gathers and the fine-stitched seams and hems. She had made them all herself.

At the bottom of the trunk was a soft rag doll, made of brown cotton cloth with black yarn hair in two braids. "Goodness," Lurie's mother said. "There's Sister! I didn't know you'd kept her all these years. I remember when I bought her, the year you were two—couldn't resist her because she reminded me so much of you. You wouldn't part with her then."

"I remember," Lurie said. "I remember Sister." She set the doll gently to one side, and began to replace the others in the trunk. "I guess," she said, "we could give these to the Salvation Army."

Her mother looked shocked. "You want to give them away?"

Lurie managed a little laugh. "Well, what am *I* going to do with them? I'm not a little girl anymore."

"I thought," her mother sounded hurt, disappointed, "you were going to save them for your children. That's what you always used to say."

"Did I?" Lurie lingered a second longer over the upturned faces looking at her forlornly from the tray of the trunk, while her mother seemed to wait for some further answer from her. Then she closed the trunk. She picked up the rag doll she had put aside. "I'm just going to keep this one," she said, and smiled a little self-consciously. "I want to give her to a little girl I know."

On the train she held Sister in her arm as she had held her

so many years ago, indifferent now to the quizzical looks of the other passengers. She would give the doll to Sabra, a belated Christmas present.

On New Years eve, Lurie and Sabra sat together on the couch, reading aloud by the light of the kerosene lamp. Together, they read lesbian novels, taking turns or reading the dialogue in parts, and they were now finishing the last chapter of this one.

Both sighed in relief that the two women in the story were still together at the end. "It's strange," Lurie finally said. "This is the third book we've read that touches on the issue of lesbian motherhood and child custody." She knew it was dangerous ground, bringing that up, and yet she was not afraid, she wanted to, tonight. She went on, "Having to choose between her child and her lover—what a choice for a woman to have to make."

"I know who I'd choose," Sabra said.

"The other woman, right?"

"Of course." Sabra smiled, seeming to have caught the safety from Lurie's mood. "You know me. It wouldn't be such a hard choice either, if the other woman was you." Then worry crossed out the smile on her face. "Who would you choose?"

"Oh...it's hard to say." Lurie tried to make it sound inconsequential, only a story they were analyzing the ending of. But she knew they were serious. She closed the book and wandered across the room, to end up staring at the little rag doll Sabra had instantly loved, who sat now looking so little in the big rocking chair.

"Who, Lurie?" Sabra's voice was insistent, cutting across the small room, then hurt. "You don't have to tell me. I know. You'd choose the little girl, wouldn't you?"

Lurie picked up the doll, turned, and recrossed the room. She put the little doll in Sabra's lap, then sat on the couch again next to Sabra and looked her full in the face. "If I had to choose ..." she said slowly. "Between a child and the woman I loved. It isn't 'If', Sabra, it's real. I've had to make that choice and I've chosen."

MARISA

There is a woman I want to write about. It seems strange for
me to try to write about her, because I hardly knew her. But I
wanted to know her much more. I even tried to know her more,
but it didn't work out that way. I want to write about her because
of the way she fascinated me and yet I never could figure her
out. Now I don't know her or see her anymore, but I'm still trying to piece it together.

I knew her name before I ever met her. Perhaps that was
what I liked first. Even that name was mysterious, intriguing,
and sounded out of place at work. Our director, Dr. Quincey,
told us he'd hired Marisa St. John as the lead teacher in the
classroom where Kathy and I are aides.

I couldn't imagine what someone with a name like that would
look like or be like. And I still don't know. Oh, I know how she
looks—right away Kathy and I tried to guess if she'd be young
or old, white or black. And Kathy was glad she was black, and
I was glad she was around my age, though that didn't seem to
help us to be friends.

Marisa was pretty, with a small, compact figure like I've
always wanted, and a smooth brown complexion that looked as
if she'd never been a teen-ager. She didn't wear make-up or
jewelry or even attractive clothes, and yet she was pretty. I
can picture her in those rust-colored corduroy slacks she wore
all the time, and those flat-heeled, round toed shoes, with her
teacher's smock over a plain turtleneck jersey.

I guess one of the first things I noticed about her was her
clothes—those corduroy pants, or a plain brown jumper and
tights—day after day. That was strange, because the place I

work is this highly professional research center and school for
disturbed children, and everyone always dresses as if they
were about to be filmed. So Marisa was noticeable for not dressing up. Even one of the kids noticed.

"How come you wear the same clothes every day?" Kim asked.
And although I'd been wondering the same thing for weeks, I
felt embarrassed for Marisa. But she didn't seem embarrassed
at all.

She looked at Kim very seriously and said, "Clothes cost a
lot of money, and everyone doesn't have money to spend on nice
new clothes. I think it's not so important to wear nice clothes as
it is to try to be a nice person, like you." And she gave Kim a
hug, who seemed satisfied.

That's what Marisa was like. She'd do strange things and
then she'd turn around and say something that made them seem
perfectly sensible. A lot of the scholarship kids, the kids whose
tuition is paid by the state, wear the same clothes every day,
too. I think Marisa did it to make a point, to say that she could
be like them, or they could be like her. But also, being a lead
teacher, she made it easier for all of us. I never felt like I could
wear pants to work until she started doing it.

Marisa did a lot of things like that. She made things change,
but not in an overpowering way—just by being herself, almost
as if she weren't aware that she was doing anything unusual.
I remember the first staff meeting that fall. All the big wheels
who condescend to talk to the classroom staff on meeting days
were there, sitting around expounding on psycho-sexual devel-
opment and ego disturbances. None of us teachers or aides ever
said too much, so everyone was surprised when Marisa challenged Dr. French about his recommendations for Vanessa.
Vanessa was a little four-year-old hurricane who would peri-
odically wreak havoc in our classroom, and Dr. French was
saying she should be put on medication. Marisa said simply, "I
don't agree with you, Joe." And that started it. In the first place,
no one ever called Dr. French "Joe." In the second place, no one
ever openly disagreed with him. And even worse, Marisa had
alternative recommendations, like behavior modification and
diet control. Dr. French was so amazed he actually let his pipe
go out while he tried to argue Marisa down. But for everything
he said, she had an answer. And when he tried to interrupt

her, she wouldn't let him.

I watched her through the whole thing. She never lost her control and she didn't even raise her voice. She just answered everything he said in a quiet, organized way, while I could hear Dr. French getting more and more agitated and flustered. But I couldn't take my eyes off Marisa. Holding her own in a situation like that—I'd never seen a woman do that before. I started really liking her. It was more than that. I began to want to be like that too. And I began to wonder why she was so different from the rest of us, and where she got her confidence, her strength.

After the meeting, I caught up with Marisa in the hall. I told her I liked the way she stood up to Dr. French, and that I agreed with what she'd said about Vanessa. Marisa said, "Thanks, Edna. I needed to hear that. It was pretty scary during that meeting. I was beginning to feel like everybody was against me."

I hadn't known Marisa was scared—she certainly didn't act like it. And I felt bad that she'd thought everybody was against her. I realized I hadn't said one word to support her, and neither had anybody else. I decided that if that ever happened at a meeting again, I wanted to say something too, to let her and all of them know that I was behind her. That short conversation was the first time Marisa had really talked to me, told me her feelings. We'd been working together for two months, and I hardly knew her. I felt bad that perhaps she didn't know I liked her, didn't know I wanted to be her friend.

Yet it was hard to be her friend, because Marisa wasn't a friendly person. She didn't seem to spend time with anybody on the staff. When a few of us got together at lunch time or during breaks, she would never be there. She seemed to disappear after work, and nobody had ever seen her outside of the school. When the office put out a mimeograph of staff addresses and phone numbers, hers wasn't on it. I knew she was new in town because I'd heard that she came in from out of town for her job interview. Perhaps she was lonely, but afraid to reach out. I thought of myself as trying to be her friend, but I didn't even know where she went for lunch.

So one week, I asked her three different times to have lunch with me. The first time she said she had reports to write, and the second time she said she wanted to go to the library during her lunch break to get books for the kids. The third time she didn't even give an excuse, and I gave up after that. Maybe she wasn't lonely and afraid, but unfriendly and anti-social.

The day she got the library books for the kids, I was looking through them, and noticed that they were all stories about black kids. It's funny, because even though a lot of the kids at the school are black, we never had many books about black kids. When Marisa read one of the books at story time one day, I had a new idea about her. Maybe she was into black power and black separatism, and that was why she was so unfriendly to me—because I'm white. If she'd been hurt a lot in her life because of being black, then of course she would be cautious and reluctant to reach out.

Right away, I wanted to talk to Kathy about it, to ask if Marisa had ever talked to her about black pride, or if Marisa was any more friendly with Kathy and the other black women than she was with me. A lot of times, the black women all eat lunch together, and sometimes they get together outside work or have parties that the rest of us aren't invited to. Maybe Marisa had been hanging out with them, and I just didn't know it.

The first chance I got to ask Kathy was at the big staff Christmas party at Dr. Quincey's house. Marisa was the only full-time staff member who wasn't there. Kathy was there with her husband, Kent, and I was with Fred, my boyfriend. When Kent and Fred got to talking about motorcycles, I told Kathy my new explanation for Marisa's unfriendliness. Kathy had been thinking just the opposite. She'd also noticed how Marisa was never friendly and at first thought it was just her, but then she'd talked to the other black women on the staff, and concluded that Marisa must not like other blacks. They'd figured Marisa thought she was too good for them, since she had a master's degree and they were all just aides or secretaries. So apparently, Marisa's aloneness had nothing to do with white or black. Kathy and I were both wrong.

Kathy said she found Marisa's attitude hard to take. "Even if it's nothing personal," Kathy said, "I can't be comfortable with her. She's a good teacher and she's good with the kids. But I always feel like she's thinking things about me she isn't saying, as if she's got all these secrets to herself, closed up in her mind." I didn't feel that way. I mean, I did feel like there was a whole lot that Marisa thought, that she never let on. But I couldn't help respecting her, admiring her. Maybe I liked her more because she didn't tell everybody everything.

All that winter, I used to look forward to going to work. The rest of my life was at an all-time low. My best friend had gotten married the summer before and moved out to the suburbs, and while I was happy for her, I really missed her. Also, things weren't going very well with Fred. It seemed as if we never had fun together any more, but were always having fights. Sometimes I'd be glad to go to work just to get away from the things that brought me down. And I looked forward to being with Marisa. Even though she never talked to me personally, as she had that one time, I felt like I was learning a lot from her—not just about teaching, but about a different way to be, to approach life.

Marisa would react to the most ordinary situations in the most extraordinary ways. Like the incident in the doll corner. It was always the little girls who used that corner, getting dressed up and playing mother. I'd learned from my training that that was good for them, to try out the adult role. But Marisa kept saying it shouldn't be like that, with only the girls in the doll corner, and the boys always playing with blocks and trucks. She'd try to get the girls to use the trucks and blocks, but of course they were never interested.

So one day, little Mark Washington, who's the youngest in our class, went over to play in the doll corner. None of us really noticed until we heard him shouting, "O.k. I'm the mommy now, so alla you shut up!" I turned around to see Mark strutting around in a long skirt, high heels, and jewelry. He looked pretty funny and I didn't think to do anything but laugh. Then Marisa and Kathy saw, and Kathy was horrified. She rushed in and stripped all those things off him, and hustled him over to the blocks. Marisa didn't say anything, but I'd never seen a look on her face like the one that was there, and I knew she was angry.

As soon as the kids were gone, Marisa exploded. "It's wrong," she said, "that the little girls get dressed up and play mothers and housewives every day, but as soon as a boy does it we get all uptight. Maybe the boys *should* get a chance to see what that feels like."

Kathy was just as upset as Marisa. "Not if I'm going to work in this classroom. I know Mark's mother, and if she knew we were letting him get dressed up like a girl, she would yank him right out of this school. It's just not right," Kathy went on. "Trying to act all cute and sexy—no boy needs to do that."

"You're right, Kathy," Marisa said, to my surprise. "The boys don't need to do that, and neither do the girls. Nobody needs to learn how to act cute and sexy, and this school is bad enough without us teaching that in the doll corner." Then Marisa talked about a whole lot of things that I'd never seen as related, before. She said we teach kids sex roles all the time —in the books and pictures we use and the activities we encourage for different kids. We teach that girls should be clean and quiet and sit down a lot, and be good all the time, while we let boys be noisy and energetic and be bad sometimes. She talked about how all the doctors and supervisors on the staff are men, while all the teachers are women, and said the kids could pick that up. She said we should make it a priority not to be constantly teaching the girls different lessons from the boys. And then she stopped and said, "I'm sorry. I guess I can get carried away on that subject. I'm not angry at either of you, Kathy or Edna. I'm angry at the whole social system. But I guess we should talk about the doll corner."

I could see the point Marisa was making, and I said maybe we ought to just get rid of the doll corner altogether. Kathy didn't agree, but said she just couldn't go along with letting boys get dressed up in women's clothing. And Marisa came up with a solution. She asked Kathy if her husband had any old clothes he could donate for the boys to dress up in. And I wondered why we'd never had those things before.

The next day at lunch, Kathy was telling the teachers from other classrooms the story about Mark and the doll corner, and ended it by saying, "I've figured out what that Marisa is up to: Women's Lib!"

Of course. That was why Marisa got so upset about the doll corner and "sex roles" in the classroom. It also explained why Marisa called all the psychiatrists by their first names, why she argued with Dr. French. And why she wasn't friendly with any of the rest of us. We were all too old-fashioned, too "sexist." In fact, all of us were married or had boyfriends. That was another thing Kathy brought up. She said, "Maybe I'll invite Marisa the next time I have a party. Kent has some fine-looking friends that'll make her forget all about being liberated."

I don't know if Kathy ever invited Marisa to one of her parties. If she did, I'm sure Marisa didn't go, or we would have heard about it from Kathy. But I did start to wonder how Marisa made out in relationships with men. I thought it must be different being a liberated woman, and everything about Marisa was different anyway. Sometimes, when I had arguments with Fred, I used to try to imagine how I would answer if I were Marisa.

One week in February, Fred and I had the worst fight we had ever had. He wanted to go to law school, and he had applied to some schools in California. Finally I brought up the question of what would happen between us if he went to school in California. Because it sounded as if he was planning to break up with me. But he kept insisting he wasn't. And I said I wasn't going to sit around writing letters to him, and I wasn't going to follow him out to California, either, unless he was planning to marry me. And that's what the fight was about. In spite of all our differences, I did want him to ask me to marry him, and it made me feel awful that he didn't even seem to be considering it. By Monday morning, we hadn't made up, and I was still upset when I went to work.

That day, classes started late because of the last big snowstorm of the year, which had ended the night before. Kathy didn't come in till late, either, and Marisa and I had a lot of free time together. While we were cutting out magazine pictures for collages, I decided to tell her my troubles. If she was into women's liberation, she would be sure to be interested in problems with men. So I told her the whole story. I got all wrapped up in it and forgot to keep cutting out pictures. But Marisa went right on with what she was doing, and when I was finished talking, she didn't say anything.

So I asked, "What would you do, if your boyfriend felt like that?"

She smiled. "I've never had a boyfriend who felt like that."

"But if you did, how would you deal with it?"

Marisa looked a little irritated, and then sighed. She knew I wouldn't leave her alone until she gave me some kind of answer. "I think," she said, "I'd try to be very careful who I got into a relationship with. And I'd make sure that they were as serious as I was, and understood what my expectations were. Do you think we've got enough pictures?"

For once, I was frustrated with Marisa. She made it sound
so easy, as if she'd never even had the littlest fight with a boyfriend. I was disappointed as well as annoyed. From a women's
liberationist, I'd expected a lot more insight and understanding.

Often, it felt like Marisa's life was a big mystery, as if all
she'd ever let us see was the surface, the role she played as a
teacher. Everything else was private. The more she wouldn't
respond, the more I wanted to know about her. For some reason,
I had let her become very important to me, and I couldn't stop
wondering about her, wanting to find out—what?

I hadn't forgotten that day, after the first staff meeting, when
Marisa had felt like everyone was against her, and how I'd
promised myself, if I had another chance, I would speak up for
her right in the meeting. But at other meetings, when Marisa
had challenged people, she'd always had plenty of arguments
and hadn't seemed to need me. So I wasn't ready when my opportunity came, at the March staff meeting. This time, the con-
troversy was about Trina Evans, a little girl in our class, and
about removing her from her home because Trina's mother
was living openly as a lesbian. Dr. French gave his usual ten-
minute monologue on the case, and was already discussing
how we could get the evidence we needed for the welfare de-
partment when Marisa broke in.

"We need to explore the whole case more," Marisa said,
"before singling out this one factor as the cause of Trina's
problems. We might even want to look more closely at Trina's
relationship with her mother."

I could see Dr. French getting hyper, since psychiatrists seem
to think they're the only ones who're qualified to talk about
kids' relationships with their mothers. But before he could interrupt, Marisa went on. "Trina and her mother seem to have
a really sound, healthy relationship, and Dianne Evans is one
of the few parents who really participates here—she comes to
all the conferences and volunteers in the classroom all the
time. We should be considering the quality of parenting, rather
than the private life of the parent. And we should hear from
other staff members who see Trina and her mother every day."

I realized with a shock that that was my opening, and· I
stumbled in. "Marisa's right about Mrs. Evans," I said. "She

does take good care of Trina, and she really seems to love her. When she comes into the classroom she always hugs Trina and talks to her, but she doesn't ignore the other kids, either. In fact, she really seems to understand little kids. She seems like a good mother to me, and I guess, well, even if she is a homosexual, does that mean Trina ought to be taken away from her?"

Right away, Dr. French challenged me. Of course, he put it all in psychiatric terms, saying he realized it would be difficult for people whose training was in education to have a full understanding of the psychopathology of homosexuality or deviant behavior. He went on and on, knowing I wouldn't understand half of what he said. When he was finished, I didn't have any answers. I didn't much care about the psychopathology of homosexuality—I'd only been trying to back Marisa up so she wouldn't feel like everybody was against her. And I looked over at Marisa, expecting her to be ready with all the answers I didn't have. But Marisa only said, "I think we should postpone the rest of this discussion until the Evans' social worker can come to a meeting."

We discussed another case after that, but Marisa didn't say anything else for the rest of the meeting. I wondered why she had stopped the discussion that way, since I was sure she had plenty of arguments. Was she finally getting tired of arguing with the psychiatrists? It didn't seem like her, and I was curious to see what she would do at the next meeting.

At the beginning of the next staff meeting, a month later, Marisa announced that she was leaving at the end of June. All of us were surprised. She hadn't told any of us anything—but then, did she ever? As soon as I had a chance, I asked Marisa about why she was leaving, and if it was anything Kathy or I had done that had made her unhappy with the job. She said no, it was nothing anyone had done, and she wasn't unhappy with the job at all. But that she and a friend had been planning, for a long time, to travel together in Europe, and that they'd finally saved up enough money to be able to do it this year.

That was the most information Marisa ever told me about her life. In spite of working with her for a year, she was still capable of surprising me. While her plans sounded exciting, Marisa seemed so sensible that I was surprised she would place traveling in Europe with a friend ahead of a good-paying job like hers. Then it occurred to me that she must be in love. The obvious explanation was that this "friend" was the man she loved. Maybe she wasn't just planning to travel in Europe. Maybe it was to be a honeymoon. Marisa would never tell us even that. But I was happy for her, if she'd found a man to love. I tried to picture what he might be like, and just couldn't. She just seemed so self-assured and confident, so calm and strong, that I couldn't picture the man who would be an equal to that. I remembered what she had said when I told her about the fight with Fred, and I decided that whoever the man was, if Marisa had chosen him, he must be pretty special. Whatever was going on in her life, I thought, I would never know. I would probably never know more about her than I knew right then.

The next year at work was very different. Susan, the new lead teacher, is not at all like Marisa. I like her, too, and we've become good friends. But even a teacher I can be friends with is no substitute for Marisa.

Fred and I broke up after he got accepted at a law school in Los Angeles. Since then, I've spent a lot of time alone. All that winter, being at home depressed me because it reminded me of Fred. So as soon as the weather turned warm that spring, I got into taking long walks on the parkway, after work and on weekends.

One of those days, I noticed a couple about half a block ahead of me, walking slowly with their arms around each other's waists and looking as though they were very much in love. Since I've been alone, I always seem to notice couples like that. A lot of times, it seems like everyone in the whole world has someone except for me. I stared at the backs of the two figures in faded blue jeans and flannel shirts, and as I got closer to them, there seemed to be something different, strange about this couple. As I came closer I realized what it was. They were the same size, built the same—they were both women. As they turned onto a path leading into the park, I could see that one woman had freckles, and unruly brown curls all around her face. And the other woman—was Marisa.

NEXT SATURDAY

The afternoon was half over and Jennifer was exhausted by the sticky June heat, the atmosphere of tension and anxiety which pervaded the room, and the strain of listening, comparing, evaluating. She made notes on the application form of the student she had just heard—a promising young man from Newbury Prep who played the violin well, but was not outstanding. None of them was outstanding. It was going to be difficult to choose this year's scholarship recipient. She flipped to the next application, glanced at her colleague to be sure he was finished making notes, and called out the name of the next student.

"Kacey Cosgrove!" As the student approached the front of the room, Jennifer was surprised. Despite the unusual spelling, she had expected Kacey Cosgrove to be a boy. But it was a little girl, in a plain striped blouse and cotton skirt, who now stood before her as Jennifer verified the information on the sheet. Yes, she was seventeen, a senior at South End High School, had studied violin for nine years. Her address and music teacher's name were correct. There was nothing particularly striking about her—gray eyes and shoulder-length brown hair that fell loose on both sides of her face. Jennifer nodded to her to begin playing scales.

After only a few measures, Jennifer's attention was caught. The girl seemed to have a confidence, a strength, an ease in her handling of the instrument that was evident even in these basic scales. Jennifer listened with her head bent, then gestured to the girl to stop, and turned to a more complex exercise. Again, she was struck by the skill. She asked the girl to play the piece she had prepared. Jennifer had heard the Mendelssohn Concerto in E Minor played by other students today, but this time it was different. This time it did not sound like a lesson, an exercise, but like a piece of music. As the girl guided the instrument unfalteringly through all the intricacies of the piece, Jennifer turned to watch her. The little girl was alive with the music she created. Her carriage was as taut and attentive as a dancer's. Her face, in its frame of brown hair, was alight, aglow. And the expression in the gray eyes was tender, almost loving. Jennifer stared at that face and wondered how she could have thought this little girl looked ordinary. She was beautiful.

For once, this year, there was no dissension among those who were judging the scholarship applicants on violin. Kacey Cosgrove was the undisputed winner. Jennifer offered to be the one to give her private lessons, which would begin during the summer. In the few weeks before Kacey's lessons began, Jennifer found herself unusually curious about this little girl. She kept thinking of her as a little girl, had to remind herself that Kacey was seventeen, and had studied the violin since she was eight. There was other information about her, too, on the application blank which Jennifer re-read in full. She learned that music had been Kacey's only outstanding subject in school. Of course, South End High was not the most ideal place to prepare for a higher education—most of its students were in vocational or business training and there had never, as far as Jennifer could remember, been a scholarship winner from that school before.

The information about Kacey's family background seemed more typical of the neighborhood she came from—a broken family, mother's occupation: L.P.N. No money to pay for college educations. If the scholarship had been based on need, Kacey would deserve it. How had Kacey reacted when she opened the letter announcing that she had won? Jennifer wished she could have been there. Had Kacey smiled, laughed, shouted to other members of her family? Had she cried? That was what Jennifer had done, twenty years ago now, when she'd received notice of her acceptance at Juilliard.

The Saturday of her first lesson, Kacey arrived looking much the same—a schoolgirl blouse and skirt, knee socks and loafers. Jennifer asked the usual questions about what she had studied, parts she had played in orchestras, what piece she was working on now. And again, when Kacey played, there was that unmistakable skill and talent. Jennifer thought with a flood of anticipation that this was exactly the kind of student she liked most to work with, one who would be able to take in all that Jennifer could give, and return as much in the gratification that came from teaching her. Then, too, as Kacey played, that irresistible loveliness again took hold of her face, and Jennifer found that she liked watching her as much as listening to her.

When the hour was over, Jennifer was reluctant to let the lesson end. As she watched the girl replace her violin in its case and gather up her music, Jennifer said suddenly, "Congratulations on winning the scholarship, Kacey." Caught by surprise, Kacey's face lit up. It was the first time Jennifer had seen her smile. She would have liked to go on talking, perhaps asking questions. But another student would be waiting, and already Kacey stood at the door of the studio. Jennifer could only say, "Next Saturday, then, at three."

As the weeks passed, Jennifer found herself looking forward more and more to Kacey's lessons. Each week she would be impressed and challenged anew by Kacey's skill and by the progress she was making. And each week, Jennifer grew more aware of the appeal Kacey held for her. In her extra time, Jennifer had been working on a new composition—a piece for two violins. It was now completed, and she felt unusually satisfied with it. Despite its apparent simplicity, it seemed a more daring, honest expression of herself than anything she had yet written. Often, she and and others of the music school staff would share original compositions, play them with each other. But for this piece, she had another idea.

At the end of Kacey's next lesson, Jennifer pulled out the completed composition. "I have something a little different I'd like you to start working on," she told Kacey. "It's a piece for two violins and I want you to work on the first part." As Kacey took the xeroxed pages with a puzzled, questioning expression, Jennifer explained, "It's one of my own compositions."

"You wrote it?" Kacey stared at her in awe, then tentatively fingered the pages.

"Don't worry about it," Jennifer reassured, marking off a measure on the second page. I just want you to try it up to here, see what you can do with it. It's not difficult." Kacey looked dubious, but she tucked the piece carefully into her portfolio, along with her exercises.

During the following weeks, Kacey worked diligently on the piece until the Saturday came when she was ready to play it through with Jennifer. As they played together, Jennifer forgot to watch and listen for faults in Kacey's technique. She was experiencing the music of herself, exactly as she had meant it to sound, expressed through Kacey. Jennifer felt that she was reaching Kacey, communicating with her, telling her things through the music that no words could have ever told. And Kacey was responding. It was like playing a game with a well-practiced teammate, like singing in close harmony with a friend you trusted never to lose the melody; it was like it had been playing music with Christina long ago.

As they reached the final note, their eyes met, and Jennifer knew from Kacey's flushed face and sparkling eyes that she had felt the same thing. Jennifer wanted to hug Kacey, wanted to say—What fun! Aren't we wonderful? But Kacey was not Christina. Kacey was the student and Jennifer must become the teacher again, assign the lesson for the next Saturday, and say good-bye.

Jennifer had already begun to sense that what she felt for Kacey was more than just the excitement and gratification of teaching a talented young student. But that lesson marked a turning point for her. She was in love.

It was not the first time. She had had crushes, infatuations, had fallen in love before. All of the people she had loved had been women. A woman—it was strange to think of this little girl that way. The others had been women already, close to her in age. She had never felt this for a student, a girl twenty years younger than herself. It was like a schoolgirl crush on a teacher, only, ironically, she felt like the schoolgirl and not the teacher.

She realized she would have to be very careful not to let her feelings be known, and not to be responsible for encouraging in Kacey any feelings for her. That was not new. She had learned, through the years of her career, to watch and listen and love from a distance, perhaps without even knowing or speaking to the object of her love. She had learned to love without expecting that love to be actualized or fulfilled. Or, if so, only in brief episodes that remained separated from the rest of her life, her work. She had learned all this early and painfully, through the one love that had been lived out to its fullest extent. She knew that she could not take this seriously. But she also knew how to take someone she loved, very seriously into her private life, her daydreams, her fantasies, where it was safe to admit her feelings and indulge in them.

She began to allow herself to fantasize about Kacey. She pictured Kacey's hands, the small deliberate fingers that Jennifer had sometimes placed in position on the strings, the bow. She would feel those fingers touching her—brushing her hair, or fastening a necklace at the back, lingering against her skin. Or she would imagine an elaborate scene—the two of them performing together for a filled house at Carnegie Hall. Before the concert, there would be a dozen white roses for Kacey. There would be no card, but Kacey would know they were from her. And for Jennifer, there would be a single red rose. And she would pin it to her breast. . . .

Now each week seemed to build up to Saturday. When Kacey came for her lessons, Jennifer would watch the tenderness and care with which Kacey handled her instrument, and think of the time, dedication, and devotion invested in Kacey's music. And wish all of that were for her. She wished there were some way to know more of Kacey, but that was dangerous. There was nothing more she needed to know, anyway. She didn't need reasons, justifications for feeling the way she did.

With fall came the start of classes at the music school. Jennifer thought about the pressure of the courses that lay before Kacey, and wondered how she would fare. She knew Kacey would be expected to keep up in classes besides music, subjects in which her high school grades were nothing to be proud of. Jennifer's concerns were increased by one lesson in particular. On that Saturday, Kacey made repeated mistakes, and Jennifer noticed that her hand shook as she handled the bow. In the middle of the lesson, Jennifer stopped her and said, "I think we'd better quit for today. Maybe you need to practice more."

Kacey looked as if Jennifer had slapped her. "But I *have* practiced. Every day this week."

"Then is something upsetting you? You look as if there's something wrong. What is it?" As Kacey hesitated, Jennifer found

herself holding her breath. —Is it anything I've done?—she
wanted to ask.

And Kacey blurted out, "It's just that my mother's been driv-
ing me crazy."

"About practicing? About your music?" Jennifer was still
worried.

"No, about stupid stuff. How I dress and who my friends
are—stuff like that."

Jennifer sighed in amused relief. How well she remembered
those painful years of adolescence. How glad she had been to
go away from home to music school. But it wasn't fair to Kacey
not to take this seriously. "I see," she said quietly. "Have you
thought about moving out, getting your own place?"

"All the time, but I won't be eighteen till January. Anyway,
how could I support myself and go to music school, too?"

How indeed? Jennifer's family had paid generously for her
tuition as well as an ample spending allowance. But there were
no such resources available to Kacey. For a brief second, Jennifer imagined inviting Kacey to come and live with her, to the
lovely old brownstone with her spacious apartment that was
often so lonely. But that was out of the question.

Kacey still stood before the music stand, clutching her violin
and bow in a grip of tension. Jennifer moved to her, and gently
took the instrument to put it in the open case. As she did so,
she felt a shock of electric fire where her finger had brushed
Kacey's, that ran through her entire body. Had Kacey felt that,
too? Trying to appear calm, Jennifer asked, "Is there anything
special you want to do with the rest of our time? Look through
some music or listen to any recordings?"

Kacey said, "I was thinking, since I'm in town, I might go
visit a friend who lives near here. If you don't mind. . . ."

"No, of course not. It'll probably be good for you." And Jennifer stifled her disappointment at being cheated out of half of
the hour she had looked forward to all week. Visit a friend.
Undoubtedly the friend mother didn't approve of. The depth of
Jennifer's feelings surprised her.

The following week, Kacey appeared for her lesson dressed
in faded blue jeans, a cotton work shirt, and dirty sneakers. So
mother gave in—Jennifer thought with delight. She admired
Kacey for having the strength and perseverance to win this

battle, and she liked the new image. Kacey as a tough street urchin. A dissenter, a rebel. Looking again, Jennifer realized that Kacey was changing anyway. She no longer appeared a little girl; that confidence and self-assurance which had previously been present only when she was playing, had begun to reside in her face, her whole body, all the time now.

Each week, Kacey's new style seemed to show more contempt for society, for convention. Patches appeared on the jeans, and her hair grew longer, wilder. So many times, Jennifer longed to brush it from her face as Kacey bent over her music. So many times, she longed to say—whatever it is you no longer have respect for, you're disgusted with, you want to reject, don't let it be the music. Keep loving the music if you have to be angry at the whole rest of the world.

But she worried. Because she was seeing a change in Kacey's lessons. Sometimes Kacey would play well, but with increasing frequency there were lessons that went badly and for which, Jennifer had to conclude, Kacey had not practiced. Often, too, Kacey seemed upset, and Jennifer wondered if there were some more serious problem in her life than a typical stormy adolescence. As she studied her during the lessons, Kacey sometimes seemed to Jennifer like an old friend she couldn't quite place. There was something familiar in her manner, her style. The work shirt had given way to a green army jacket, the sneakers to boots, as early fall gave way to November. Kacey would now come in to her lessons with her cheeks red from the cold. Her fingers would be so numb she would not be able to play for the first five or ten minutes. She would look as if she had been outdoors all day, and Jennifer wondered what she did with her Saturday mornings, how she spent the rest of her life.

One day Kacey came in with her hair cut short, the wild brown tangle gone. And Jennifer suddenly knew who she was reminded of. Herself. At eighteen, when she had gone away to music school and first given in to dressing as she felt, as who she really was. Jeans and men's shirts weren't acceptable then, even far from home. But she had found tailored shirtwaists, had worn pants in her room, had even owned a pair of boots. And she, too, had cut her hair for the first time. She had dressed like that for a reason—for other women who, like herself, might be seeking love in women, and who would be able to tell she was one of them, by one look. Was Kacey, she wondered, changing her appearance for the same reason? Was she going to be the same kind of woman Jennifer had become?

At home that evening, Jennifer studied pictures of herself in an old photograph album from her college days. The clothes were different, but in her own face she saw the same defiance that she now saw in Kacey's face. She turned the page and was startled by the enlarged photograph of Christina. In a long black gown that exposed her throat and shoulders, holding her violin in her hand—Christina, smiling. Christina, whom she tried not to think about anymore. But now she let herself remember. They had met through hearing each other play, then played together through the last two years of school. Christina had been her first lover. But it was always the music that they both loved as much as, perhaps more than each other. And just as it had brought them together, it was the music that had driven them apart.

At first, the competition was friendly, but it had grown serious, and the climax was reached when both auditioned with the same orchestra, and Jennifer got the job instead of Christina. They had tried to live together after that, but it became painful whenever Jennifer practiced. Painful when Christina left each morning for her job teaching violin lessons at the nearby elementary school, while Jennifer prepared for her rehearsals. They had broken up in a storm of fights and recriminations Jennifer did not want to remember. She closed the album.

One evening, as Jennifer was crossing the windy square on her way to a concert, she heard a man's voice call out, "Casey! Hey, Casey! Over here!" She had only to glance around to see who the man was. One of a group of young gay men that hung out by the fountain in the little park, even on the coldest days and nights. Sometimes there were a few young women among them, dressed in boots and men's jackets so that it was hard to tell them apart. Other people also frequented the square, but this crowd always stayed clearly apart, and the others did not mix with them. Tonight, Jennifer's glance took in a figure she knew well. In answer to the shout, Kacey Cosgrove was crossing the square in long strides, to join the group.

So now she knew that her suspicions about Kacey were right. As Jennifer continued across the square and toward the music hall, she was filled with intense emotions. She wondered what it would mean for Kacey, the life she was entering. Thought about what it had meant at that age for herself.

Herself—that was the thought that greedily pushed itself to center front. If Kacey was going to grow to love a woman, why not herself? She had always kept the two worlds—that of her music and that of her feelings about women—completely separate. She had moved between them convinced, in both, of the need to hide, cover up, appear not to be who she was. She had allowed Kacey to have a place in her feelings. And now that she knew Kacey was like her, she wanted to act on those feelings. But Kacey was already also firmly established in the world of her music. Kacey's classmates were Jennifer's students, her teachers Jennifer's colleagues.

And an even greater risk might lie in the possible relationship itself. She had taken such a chance with Christina, and the hurt she had suffered had caused her to make the choice she had lived out ever since. How could she take that chance again? Perhaps, with someone else, it would be different for Kacey. Perhaps Kacey would be strong enough to persevere until she found fulfillment in both worlds, in her personal life as well as her music.

As the winter deepened, it became clear that Kacey was never practicing. She would try to sight-read her lessons, stumbling through them, and Jennifer would have to re-assign the work for the following week. Jennifer knew she should talk to Kacey about her poor progress, and the possibility of having to terminate the lessons if it continued. She knew that part of her role was to deliver threats and ultimatums. And she wanted to talk. But not to deliver threats and ultimatums. More and more, she wanted to talk to Kacey about herself.

Now that she felt she knew the source of Kacey's trouble, it hurt not to be able to offer a single word of empathy. Perhaps, if Kacey knew about her, it might help her through this difficult period, and encourage her to continue to be serious about her music. The urge to open herself up to Kacey became almost an obsession in Jennifer's thoughts. She thought about how well she had kept her secret all these years, and wondered if she could now make this exception. Did she really think she could help Kacey, or were other motives behind this urge? If she were

to talk to Kacey, how much would she tell her, anyway? Only
about her past, her own adolescence, her choice of loving
women? Or did she mean to tell Kacey how she felt about her,
that she had dreams about her at night and fantasies all the
day? Would Kacey be insulted? Would she laugh at this from a
woman she undoubtedly considered old? Did she have a lover
already, another girl her age? Or was there any possibility that
she felt the same way Jennifer did?

At the start of the second semester in January, Jennifer received a call from the dean for first year students at the music
school. He wanted to talk to her about Kacey Cosgrove's progress. He was concerned because she had fallen so far behind
in her work. She had failed her English and math courses, and
even her grades in theory and composition were barely passing.
There were also numerous unexcused absences, and she had
failed to show up for one of her exams. Kacey was in danger of
losing her scholarship.

In response, Jennifer tried to plead Kacey's cause, remind-
ing the dean of Kacey's lack of resources, and how little support
her family might provide for a serious student of classical music.
She told him that she knew there were personal and family
problems. In the end, she promised to talk to Kacey, and that
promise stayed on her mind. She had to decide, now, what direction her talk would take.

That evening, she returned home late from the music school.
It was eleven by the clock in the square and a fine drizzle was
turning the snow underfoot to slush. Yet, as she approached
the fountain, she saw the remnants of the usual crowd of young
men. Nearing them, she thought how anonymous she was in
her black wool coat, her subdued gray scarf, with her leather
portfolio tucked under one arm. No one of them would ever suspect she was like them. As the figures grew sharper, she recognized Kacey—leaning slouched against the low brick wall, with
her hands in the pockets of her army jacket, her head bare,
her short hair glistening in the fine mist. Before Jennifer could
think to change her course or look the other way, Kacey had
seen her. Their eyes met for one second, neither of them spoke,
and Jennifer walked on.

Inside her warm, comfortable apartment, Jennifer wished
she had invited Kacey to come home with her. She would dry

Kacey's hair with a soft, thick towel. She would build a fire, and put on the Brandenburg Concertos, and make hot chocolate for the two of them. She would hold Kacey in her arms before the fire, and tell her that she did not need to ever be outside with no place to go, at eleven o'clock at night, again. That she could always come here. . . .

She could not go on fantasizing like this. The time had come to break all the rules she had made for herself, to break through the disguises and lies and begin to live her life honestly. Next Saturday, she would tell Kacey how she felt about her. And find out. . . .

On Saturday, she waited anxiously for three o'clock to arrive. Nervously, she paced the polished floor of her studio. As the clock from the square chimed three, she found herself impatiently scanning the street outside her windows. Kacey was always on time. But Jennifer's wristwatch registered five, then ten minutes past the hour. When it was half past three, she knew Kacey would not arrive. She felt a soft queasiness lodge in the pit of her stomach. Kacey had never missed a single lesson. What if some accident had happened to her, or some serious illness? She tried to reason with herself that other students missed lessons. Frequently, they called afterwards to explain, and perhaps Kacey would do that. Jennifer stayed at the studio an hour, two hours later than usual, but no call came.

There was no call during the week, either, and Jennifer plodded through her classes, rehearsals, and concerts with increasing anxiety and dread. All week, she walked through the square as often as possible, scrutinizing the crowd by the fountain, but she saw no sign of Kacey. When Friday came, she called the dean of the music school. Asked if he knew whether Kacey was ill, and if she'd missed any of her classes. He didn't know if she was ill, since she hadn't called. But he did know that Kacey had not attended any class for two weeks, and that her name was on the probation list. After that, there was nothing to do but wait until tomorrow, Saturday, when Kacey would surely come, and Jennifer could tell her. . . .

The next afternoon, Jennifer again waited in a fever of anxiety. Three o'clock came again, with no ring, no knock, no call. When the full hour had passed, Jennifer made telephone calls to cancel her engagements for the rest of the day and evening.

She apologized to the waiting student, saying she was ill, and
went home early.

When she reached the quiet security of her apartment, she
leafed through her portfolio to find what she wanted—Kacey's
application form which listed her home telephone number.
Jennifer could hear her own heart pounding violently as she
dialed the number, listened to the rings. A woman's voice answered the phone.

"I'd like to speak to Kacey Cosgrove."

"She's not here." The voice sounded strained, muffled, perhaps as if the woman had just woken up.

"When do you expect her?"

"Never. She doesn't live here anymore."

Jennifer tried to cover her surprise, her fear. But her voice
shook as she asked, "Can you tell me where I can reach her?"

"No, I...I don't know where she is. She's...left home. She's
gone...." The voice at the other end burst into sobs. Jennifer
listened for a few seconds to this unknown woman crying, and
then quietly replaced the receiver.

A sense of futility began to seep, like dampness, inside her.
But there must be somewhere else she could try, someone. If
only she had acted sooner. If only Kacey would...if only next
Saturday....

A SENSE OF LOSS

They said good-bye to each other at home, in an embrace of faded flannel with the severe black and white cotton print: the two heads close—Mandy's fine straight light-brown hair against the soft fluff of Liz's afro, their cheeks touching, their eyes full of tears.

"You're sure you want to go?" And Liz nodded.

"You're sure you don't want me to come with you?" Liz shook her head, her throat too full for words. (No, Mandy. I'll be o.k. It won't be heavy. I hadn't seen her for seven years anyway— I hardly knew her anymore.) No words—only their embrace that lasted until Liz's taxi came to take her to the airport to catch a plane to Graysburg for her grandmother's funeral.

The two women had lived together for one year, and this was their first real separation, the first place that one had had to go without the other. Mandy had offered to accompany Liz, but Liz could not let her do that. Everyone at the wake, the funeral would be black—all the family, relatives, friends. There would be no place for Mandy and she would stand out conspicuously, inhibiting everyone at a time when they needed to be with people among whom they felt safe. If it were a man Liz were married to, even a white man, perhaps it would be different. A husband would be family by marriage, in-law, someone who could claim a right to be there. But how could she justify the presence of the woman she loved? She could imagine how the voices would whisper, wondering, "Who's that little white girl with Elizabeth?" She could never subject Mandy to that.

Her sister swung the big blue Chevrolet that Liz recognized instantly as her parents' car into the loading-area drive. Charlotte, the sister who was safe, the only one of the family who knew about Liz and Mandy, who knew that Liz was a lesbian. They filled the first ten minutes updating each other on their lives the past few months, and Charlotte told Liz the details and circumstances of their grandmother's illness and death. Negotiating the hills and corners of Graysburg, heading toward its outskirts, Charlotte managed to survey her "little" sister critically.

As it always did under that look, Liz's mind raced with anxieties. (Am I o.k.? I know my hair's all right—I just had it cut a week ago. And this is the plainest dress I have—I know it covers my knees, even sitting down.) She gave it a tug, to be sure, then squirmed uncomfortably in the seat belt to get a good look at Charlotte. Her sister always looked so much like a suave, sophisticated model on the cover of Essence Magazine, that beside her Liz felt unkempt and disheveled. (Did I remember to put lotion on my legs? Say something, Charlotte. Tell me I look o.k. or I don't. Don't let me arrive looking outrageous and gauche even if I am. That's why I wanted you to pick me up.)

"Liz, you haven't said anything to Mom and Dad yet, have you? About. . .?"

"Me and Mandy?" So that was it. "No."

"Good." Charlotte was visibly relieved. "Don't. I don't think this would be a good time to tell them."

"For Christ's sake, Charlotte," Liz snapped angrily. "How insensitive do you think I am? You think in the middle of Grandma's funeral I'm going to decide it's the perfect time to announce to the whole family that I'm a lesbian?"

"Well, I never know about you. You're always trying to be so Creative and Different and Communicate Honestly and all that. Even why you want to tell them at all is beyond me. No, never mind," as Liz opened her mouth to reply. "You already tried to explain it to me. Anyway," she went on in a less resigned tone, "I'm glad you conceded to wear nylons and a dress."

"What'd you *think* I'd wear? Overalls and hiking boots?"

"I remember one Christmas you showed up in that bedspread thing you tried to pass off as a party dress." And they were at it again, the sweet good daughter versus the family's angry rebel, the white sheep—bantering back and forth in the typical tradition of siblings of the Free family. Inside, it made Liz smile —she could pick up the acceptance beneath that surface of sarcasm, knew it was Charlotte's way of showing affection. And anyway, Liz could usually think up sharp quips and retorts much faster than Charlotte.

Besides all the usual furniture, footstools, knickknacks, photographs, and crocheted doilies, Grandma Free's tiny living room was crowded with people—cousins, great aunts and uncles, aged friends—all of them black, all of them married, at least at some time in their lives, all of them straight. Liz became Elizabeth Joy, Greg's daughter, the youngest granddaughter— polite, cordial, solicitous, sympathetic.

"So you're Elizabeth—all grown up now. Guess you don't remember your old Uncle Alec?"

(Of course not, Uncle Alec. I wouldn't have known you from Adam.) "Of course I do, Uncle Alec. How are you?"

Individuals detached themselves from the mass and approached her with formalities, questions.

"Are you Lester's wife?"

(No, I'm Mandy's lover.) "No, I'm Marie's daughter. And Greg's." He went off, presumably in search of Lester's wife, and was shortly replaced by another.

"Elizabeth! Last time I saw you, you were only this high! But why did you cut off all that pretty hair?" For that one, she groped for an answer. They wouldn't understand that the way she wore her hair expressed her political stance, as much as it expressed her self, her pride. Or that something like short cut hair helped to make her recognizable to other women like herself. Wryly, she answered that it was the style.

"So tell me," her aunt Catherine said, "what do you do now?" She would have liked to answer: I'm a lesbian now, and live with a woman named Mandy. Or—I belong to a lesbian writers collective and write articles for the local gay newspaper. She wished she could pull it off, smiling sweetly at Aunt Catherine the whole time. They didn't know what a real radical was, didn't realize she was quite harmless. She sighed and gave the correct answers about her job and education, all the things which did not really matter.

Across the room on the piano stood a photograph of her taken
at junior high school graduation—a chubby-faced little black
girl with greasy curls and a string of pearls around her neck.
That's the one they want me to be, forever, she thought. Elizabeth Joy Free. Little Elizabeth. She turned and caught a glimpse
of herself in the full length mirror by the coat rack—the smooth
cut of the black and white print, slim brown legs, the neat, round
shape of her 'fro—nothing, in fact, to let them know she hadn't
become exactly the person that the little girl in the photo was
supposed to become. Nothing except the absence of a wedding
band. It was a good disguise, but she felt the burden of it, felt
like a first class hypocrite.

She reassured herself by thinking that, if statistics could be
believed, there were others in the room who were gay like herself. There would be, let's see, at least four. Now who could
they be? Uncle Alec? Aunt Catherine...?

As soon as she could, she slipped out of the house and up
into the steep backyard, where her grandmother's garden lay.
She had spent hours of her childhood summers in that garden.
She'd helped to weed and pick beans and mustard and kale in
the hot sun, sat in the swing under the cool grape arbor suck-
ing the sour unripe grapes from their skins. She'd picked tomatoes to ripen on the kitchen windowsill, played hide-and-seek
between the high rows of corn. She'd gone foraging, even farther
up the rocky hill to where the wild blackberries grew in a
bramble, had sacrificed bare arms and knees to scratches,
collecting enough fruit for the promised, famous blackberry pie.

Unlike the houseful of inquisitive people, the garden did not
prod her or scrutinize her or force her to lie. It was living, alive,
and it seemed to speak to her in her grandmother's voice. The
garden was like her grandma—tough, determined, resilient.
Her grandma had loved this stubborn, wild, rocky piece of
ground she had claimed from the barren hillside and cajoled
and coaxed to yield food for two generations of daughters and
sons. Being here was like being with Grandma Free. Liz could
see the brown, wrinkled, wiry old woman, bent over in a huge
sunbonnet and a gingham apron. Could feel the hard, calloused
fingers on her own bare sun-browned shoulder. Could hear
her rough, splintery voice, as she used to sometimes talk to

the vegetables:

"Now stop acting so pitiful, and grow. I ain't running no green-house here. You better get used to this poor, rocky dirt—it's all we got." She'd tug at the carrots and turnip tops. "Come on out of that ground! Don't you know those children got to have some supper?" Liz remembered the day she'd planted the apple tree. She'd closed a knotted hand around the slender trunk of the little sapling and said, "I know you're little now, but you're going to grow up real pretty and fine one day. I'm going to see that you do."

She had spoken to Liz in the same way—if the words were short sometimes, impatient, hugs were long, and her love was rich and generous.

At the back of the garden the single apple tree stood, full grown now. Liz drank in the cider-sweet scent of late summer from the full laden branches and the bounty of windfalls that covered the ground beneath it. The tree seemed so unlikely here at the edge of this patch of kitchen vegetables—apart, unique, alone. And yet, Liz felt quite sure that it had been her grandmother's pet, her favorite of all that grew here.

Only here in the garden did she begin to feel the reality of her grandmother's death, to feel the loss. And she returned to the house subdued, saddened, feeling that she too was a part of this mourning, this grieving, that this bereavement was also hers.

At the service, the chapel was full to overflowing. Liz sat beside her sister Charlotte and closed her eyes, letting it flow into her senses—heavy perfume of the flowers, slow somber chords from the pipe organ, and then the intrusion of the preacher's voice. Voice strong and full with that familiar black accent, rich and diverse as the fading tones of the organ, softened by the gentle southern overtones. That single voice, rising like a storm, falling like gentle rain. The words wove patterns of poetry, creating of her grandmother's life a legend as simple and pure as a bible story or the words to a hymn. Her goodness, her unwavering faith, her trials and small tri-umphs were captured in their own language and cadence, balanced and full.

What Liz remembered was Sundays in church as a child.

Sundays when a preacher like this one could make the people
sigh and shout and echo Amens, could move a whole congrega-
tion to tears. Sundays when she, too, was swept along on that
current of feeling, burning with the shame of sin, reaching out
to catch hold of a faith as tangible as a rock, emerging uplifted
on the tide of love that surged through the whole church as if
they all were one. This man was working the same kind of spell.
The mourners were released by this voice to express their sor-
row. Liz felt a tight ache inside her, struggling to burst. She
wanted to let this touch her, too, wanted to let go, but she felt
distant, far out of touch with the pain that was her pain, too.

Then there was music, the songs she had heard all through
her childhood—in church, in her home, even hummed under
her grandmother's breath in the garden—"I am a poor way-
faring stranger," and "Deep river, my home is over Jordan."
Those sad sweet mournful songs. She felt a surge of nostalgia.
This music was her culture, her heritage, her own voice.

She found herself thinking about Mandy—Mandy who, as a
child, had been taken on the sabbath to reserved and unemo-
tional services given in a language she didn't even understand.
Mandy had never been in a church like this one, had never
known this music. Liz felt that perhaps Mandy could never
understand this part of her, of her past. And yet how she loved
her, how she longed for her even at this minute, even here where
Mandy would be so hopelessly out of place. The sound of sobs
near her brought her attention back, and she turned to see
that Charlotte, reserved, sophisticated Charlotte, was crying, too.

The line of cars, lights on at midday, crawled slowly through
the streets to the small cemetery on the hill. Liz felt strange
to be inside the car this time, and not one of the people she saw
through the window, waiting impatiently to cross the street.
The cars pulled up on the side of the drive, and the people gathered around the open grave. The preacher said quietly the
words Liz found she had been waiting for, the words about
ashes and dust. And they watched the coffin being slowly lowered down into the earth.

Liz looked around her at the circle of faces—black, brown,
tan, pale. Her grandmother's sisters, brother, grandchildren

and a great-grandchild, nieces, nephews, children of cousins. They let their grief flow openly, and still Liz could not cry.

She wondered what her own funeral would be like. There would be no children or grandchildren for her, no family. Perhaps Mandy, perhaps a handful of friends. Perhaps, if Mandy had died already, there would be no one left who would really mourn her. She looked again round the circle, this large family of generations, strong even in their weakness, deriving their strength from each other. And she knew that, though they were her family, they were not there for her as they were for each other. She was of them, but no longer one of them. She had disinherited herself. Yet she would never lose her past, strong as she had felt it within her as she heard that music of her childhood, just as she would never forget this day, or lose this fresh sense of loss, but would carry it within her all the days of her life.

She wanted to talk, wanted to tell Mandy about it, but what could she say now that Mandy could understand? How could she explain the way she had felt in the church, the way she had felt at the side of the grave? She felt tightly strung, coiled like an overwound spring, yet felt there were no words.

When Mandy questioned her, she began to tell her about the garden. "I went up to her garden, all by myself. I used to work up there when I was a kid, and play there, too. It was so much like her, so tough and persistent and determined, on that crazy rocky hillside. It was her—much more than that. . . coffin they had in there." An involuntary shudder ran through her. She went on.

"Mandy, it was all still growing. The tomatoes were red and they were huge. Something was eating up the leaves—they were all chewed up into skeletons. *She* wouldn't have let that happen. And the squash vines were running wild over everything. And the apple tree—I was there when she planted it, and it was so little, and now it's big—the apple tree had hundreds of apples on it, and a hundred more on the ground. Just lying there, on the ground, rotting. Nobody gathered them up; nobody cared." She was quiet for several seconds, then said, "I wonder if the apple tree remembers her? I wonder if it misses her. . . too."

Mandy drew her closer and said, "We'll grow a garden, here, next spring. We'll plant an apple tree—to remember her—and we won't let anything rot or die."

And suddenly the awful sadness that was within Liz burst and broke free, and the tears came. That flood of tears that had seemed bound and plugged inside her came effortlessly, easily, the storm finally breaking. In Mandy's arms, she was able to cry.

"My grandma," she sobbed. "My grandma's dead." She cried like a child while Mandy held her close. And she knew now where her home was, her family: here in the arms of the woman who loved her, who understood.

LEFTOVERS

From the second-hand shops, they had brought home bags full of blue: denim jackets, jeans, overalls and work shirts. After supper, everything had been tried on before the full length mirror, and now lay spread in a dark and pale patchwork across the double bed. Sitting cross-legged in the center, Julia held a measuring tape against the hem of the first pair of jeans. In the corner closet, the one that was seldom opened, Gina searched for hangers. But she emerged with her arms full of brightly colored garments—a tumbled load, marked by a band of rick-rack, an embroidered ribbon, an exotic eastern design trailing in a long sweep to the floor, a shimmer of acetate—dresses. In answer to Julia's questioning look, Gina offered the explanation, "I thought, with all the new clothes, I should get rid of some of these." Then, softly, "I never wear this stuff anymore."

Julia watched from the middle of the denim patchwork, the marking chalk momentarily still in her hand. Watched Gina pull from the tumble a bright orange dress with a short full skirt and bands of shirring across the waist and bodice. "You used to wear that?"

"To dance in." Gina held the full skirt wide. "I loved the way the skirt danced when I did."

Julia shook her head, bending over to send the shears flying in a swift arc to their destination. "Nobody wears party dresses to go dancing."

"It's not a party dress. Just fun to dance in." Gina's back was turned now as she held the dress against her, watching herself in the mirror.

"Well, how come you don't?"

"Don't what?" The orange dress sailed across the room, to
land accurately atop the heap Gina had deposited on the chair.

"Don't wear it anymore? To dance in?"

Gina was back in the closet before she answered. "I guess,
you know, being with you, it would feel strange." Her voice was
muffled by the rack of clothes. "I don't think I would feel. . .
comfortable." She emerged again and began to be busy removing hangers.

Now Julia's scissors stopped in their course. "Gina—would
you like it if I liked to get dressed up, too?"

What else could she answer? She did not lie, not to Julia.
"Yes, I would. Of course I would. It's fun, sometimes. My friend
Sharon and I used to do that—get dressed up for no reason and
maybe go buy ice cream cones. It was fun." She and Sharon
had worn skirts to the floor and broad-brimmed straw hats.
They had pretended to be Ursula and Gudrun from *The Rain-
bow*. They'd buy ice cream and sit on a bench on the parkway.
Sharon would watch all the men who passed. Gina would watch
Sharon—Sharon wearing ribbons and flowers around the
crown of her wide-brimmed hat. "But I would never ask you to
do that."

"Oh, I would never do it." Julia fingered the frayed edge of a
pair of jeans, picked at the fine threads. "But *you* could."

And what would everyone think, Julia? With me in a long skirt
and a summer straw hat, and you in jeans and a belt and boots?
You know what they'd think. She continued to strip the clothes
from their hangers and answered, "I don't mind not doing those
things now. It's the past." Like wanting a wedding. Like expecting that some day someone else would pay for her hats and
shoes and dresses. Like wanting a baby she could array in ribbons and flowers. Another door in her mind swinging shut, the
latch clicking.

Working through the pile, she had reached a turquoise colored
skirt with a deep ruffled flounce at the hem. She remembered—
she'd worn it the night she and Sharon had gone to the Town
Edge to hear the bouzouki players and dance the syrtos. Coming
home, they had missed the last bus and it had started to rain.
Sharon and Gina had walked four miles in the pouring rain,
carrying their sandals slung over their shoulders, and lifting
their skirts for the puddles, laughing and singing. The past.

"It still makes you feel bad, doesn't it?" Julia asked, her eyes on the needle she was threading with blue. Without waiting for an answer she went on, "You don't have to get rid of anything if it makes you feel so bad. Not on my account."

Gina paused, studying Julia's bent-over head. The bright skirt alone remained in her hands. "Of course it makes me feel bad. A lot of things I remember make me feel bad." She would feel bad, and allow herself that. Not too bad—she wouldn't cry. She wasn't sorry. Just feel bad enough to maybe write a poem. "I don't mind feeling bad," she said.

Julia had stopped, too. Now she pushed the jeans she had been altering swiftly aside. The scissors clattered to the floor. "Gina. Maybe you should have stayed straight. All the things you miss —getting dressed up and going out and stuff—you'd have been much happier straight. You could have a big fancy wedding, and then you could have a kid and stay home and indulge your-self in self-pity all week, waiting for some man to take you out dancing on weekends—all dressed up."

Gina froze as the words sliced into her, plunged to her soft center, pierced her most vulnerable place, that ineradicable past when she was still straight. Julia would know how much that hurt. The tears Gina had transcended only minutes before now suddenly filled in. She turned abruptly, the blue skirt still caught in her hands, and left the room. Shut the door behind.

In the small extra room that was next to their bedroom, she held the turquoise cloth to her face, rubbed her fingers in the fabric, feeling the gloss, crushing the gathers in her hands. Julia, I won't be sorry for the way my life was before I met you. You have no right to judge that. You don't know what it was like to be straight. Maybe I did care a lot about pretty dresses and believe a lot of pretty lies. But there was much more to it than that.

The turquoise skirt fell in deep folds across her lap. There used to be beads—blue beads that matched the skirt. They must be here in this room, in the little chest that was also stuffed full of leftovers. The jewel box. She got up and began to search through the drawers of the chest. Yes, in the corner, the jewel box, in the bottom, a fold of yellowed tissue-paper. She drew them out.

The blue beads shone in her fingers, clicked softly into a

mound against the matching fabric—deeper blue than the sky after a rainfall. They were real turquoise, held together by tiny links of silver wire. Sharon had sent them to her from Mexico. Gina had been shocked when she unwrapped the little package— the beads were too valuable, too expensive, too unlikely a purchase for Sharon, trying to last out a year in Mexico on a pauper's budget. And a month later, Gina had had to wire Sharon the money to get home.

Where was Sharon now? After the Mexico episode, Gina's memories of her were distant, cloudy. For Sharon there had been a marriage, an alcoholic husband; for Gina, heart-rending letters from her, long distance phone calls at three a.m. Could Sharon come and stay with her? Gina always said no. No, Sharon, it's too late now. It wouldn't be the same any more. You wanted to be his wife. I wanted you to be my friend. . . . After a time, the letters and calls had stopped.

She folded the skirt and scooped up the handful of turquoise beads. I won't lie to you Julia. I'll try to explain it to you—what it was I valued, and why I can't let you rob me of my past. . . . She left the skirt where it lay, but carried the beads back with her to the bedroom. She could talk to Julia now.

But the room was dark. The new clothes had been pushed to a crumpled heap on the floor, and there was a small mound under the quilt on the double bed. Gina sat down softly beside it and drew back the edge of the quilt. Julia was asleep—curled into a knot, fast in her familiar escape from hurt, from pain. Gina sat still for a long time watching her. Julia's eyes were shut, the lashes still against her cheek, her mouth slightly open. One arm and hand were exposed, the fingers clenched in a fist shoved deep into the pillow. She looked so small—so still. I don't want you to go away from me like that, Julia. You don't have to hide from me and keep on hurting. Did I hurt you that much? How much?

Gina leaned over and brushed a wisp of curl from Julia's cheek. She let the blue beads hang from her hand, over the side of the bed, then let them go. She kissed the round curve of Julia's shoulder, her temple, kissed the hollow at her throat.

A MONOGAMY STORY

The night before, they had not made love. They had lain still, holding each other for a long time in the silence, until Sima had asked, "Emmy, are you still awake?"

"Just barely." She tried to focus in, be coherent. "Why? What are you thinking about?"

"I don't know. Worrying, I guess."

"About the weekend? About me going away?"

"Maybe." There was a pause, then Sima went on. "Sometimes I get worried that things are changing between us. Sometimes I'm not sure how you feel about me...."

"*That* isn't going to change," Emily reassured her. "I still love you."

"Do you?"

Emily held her tightly, "You know I do." Sima returned the hug, but in the darkness, Emily wished she could see her face, could be certain that Sima believed it. She had intended to stay awake, to ask more questions or listen some more, but in Sima's arms, it was too easy to fall asleep. In the morning, she had forgotten the conversation like a dream.

There wasn't time for a proper goodbye. They were late, as they always were, and Emily had to run the last half block as she saw the airport bus approaching the corner, Sima running behind with the small bag that held Emily's sleeping bag and change of clothes. They had a few seconds to hug and kiss each other one more time, while a confused-looking man with several suitcases asked the bus driver for information. "I'll miss you," Sima said.

"I'll miss you, too. I love you." Then the bus was pulling away and Emily dropped her change in the box and looked around for a seat. By the time she could see out the window, the bus was too far down the block. Sima had to go back to work: she had taken her lunch hour to see Emily off. Emily had taken the whole day off, in order to be in Chicago for the Lesbian Writers Conference, which began that evening.

She stared out the cloudy bus window into the cloudier day beyond, without really seeing the familiar sights. She was aware only of being taken farther and farther away from Sima. They had been together for a year now, and had never been away from each other for longer than a night. Now, Emily would be in Chicago for two nights and three long days, alone.

She had lots of time between here and the airport to think about what she was doing and why—what it would be like to be away from Sima, and at a conference with all those other women. She loved Sima immensely. She was sure of that. In the time that they had been lovers, they had always chosen to be together, passing up activities that only one or the other was interested in doing. This was the first time that pattern had intentionally been broken. But, for a long time now, Emily realized uncomfortably, she had been aware of a growing restlessness, a nudging curiosity.

It had to do with lesbianism. Sima was her first female lover, the one who had brought her out. (Emily smiled to herself thinking how she'd learned the lingo now; perhaps no one would guess she'd been straight only a year ago.) From the time they became a couple, theirs was a traditional relationship which evolved naturally into living together. It wasn't that she was not happy living with Sima, happy with their home. She loved the cozy, compact apartment, that often reminded her of the playhouses she had fantasized as a child—Sima the perfect playmate to keep house with. It was just that she kept feeling this restlessness, this doubt, this curiosity.

She suspected that her own knowledge of lesbianism was really very limited. She had never been in a women's bar. The few friends that she and Sima had were quiet couples like themselves. Emily had had other friends before—they were still straight, and now she felt little in common with them. Sima's former friends were lesbians, all right. But, even though she never said so, it was clear that now she didn't want to spend time with women who were single.

Still, Emily knew, if only from hearsay, that there were other lesbians who lived very differently from her and Sima. Somewhere, she had read something by a woman who didn't believe in monogamy, who called it a product of the patriarchy, a form of oppression. And supposedly, some gay women were completely promiscuous, picking each other up in bars. She had also heard about communes, collectives, and lesbian communities where women's lives crossed and criss-crossed, where everyone had been everyone else's lover at one time or another.

Whenever she tried to talk to Sima about these things that she read or heard, Sima would seem reluctant. Sometimes, Emily would ask how things were different for lesbians five or ten years before, what the bars were like, or whether there was any accuracy to the accounts of gay life given by those old paperback novels. Sima's answers would be vague and unenlightening; inevitably she would change the subject.

It happened so often that Emily began to suspect that Sima felt threatened. She couldn't tell why. Was the fear that, if Emily knew more about different ways to live, she would find them so wonderful that she would change her mind about being with Sima? Were they, then, so wonderful? Sima's reticence only made her more curious.

Then the news of the Lesbian Writers Conference had come up. Emily was a poet. Her work had changed radically since her identification with lesbianism, but she had not found other writers she could share her new work with, or who could give her the feedback she needed. The thought of a gathering of fifty or maybe even a hundred lesbian writers in one place at one time was overwhelming. She had to be there. At first, they had considered that they both might go to the conference, as they had gone everywhere together for the past twelve months. But Chicago was far away—too far to reach by bus or train in one weekend. To fly there cost over a hundred dollars for just one fare—they couldn't afford two. Anyway, Sima was not a writer.

So they had agreed that only Emily would go. The decision had been made weeks ago, and on the surface it made perfect sense. But beneath the surface, Emily knew that Sima did not want her to go—not alone. And in her own mind, on a level that was just conscious, she knew that this was the chance she'd been waiting for.

Sometimes, she wondered if she and Sima were together only because Sima was the first woman she had ever made love with. A pang of guilt accompanied this thought. But what would it have been like if she'd known she was a lesbian years ago, if she'd had opportunities to be with lots of other women? Would she still be with Sima now? This weekend, apart from Sima, would she find out?

The driver was calling out the names of airlines. She fished for her pocketwatch, wondering if the hour that this ride took could already be over. "TWA!" That was her stop. Hastily gathering together her knapsack and the small blue bag, she made her way off the bus and into the terminal. She had flown many times before, knew how to navigate an airport. But it seemed like a lifetime since she had been anywhere or undertaken anything difficult without Sima at her side. As she boarded the plane, it felt like her first flight all over again.

Sitting by the window on the plane, watching the layers of gray clouds falling below, she was seized with panic. The last time they'd flown, it was Sima who was frightened. Emily had held her hand and made up silly guessing games until Sima could laugh at her own fears. There was nobody now to take Emily's mind off the flight. At every change in the engine's sound, every dip and rise and pocket of air turbulence, her heart raced. What if the plane blew up, or collided with something in these clouds, or the motor failed? What if she could never get home to Sima again?

Gratefully, she accepted coffee from the flight attendant and tried to turn her mind to other thoughts. The conference. She'd be alone there, too. But wasn't that exactly what she wanted? She'd been alone many times before—most of her life. But that was different—it was when she was straight. She'd never had a chance to be alone as a lesbian. Somewhere at the back of her mind was always a persistent worry about whether she was a real lesbian, or only Sima's lover. Would the women at the conference accept her at face value? They wouldn't know she was Sima's or anyone else's lover. She could be whoever she wanted to be.

Finding her way through Chicago was more impossible than the most confusing airport. She got lost once and later got on the wrong subway train. To keep up her confidence, she played a game: because she was a lesbian, she could do anything. Finding her way alone through the nightmare and perils of a dangerous foreign city—a task to make a heterosexual woman immobile with fear—was mere child's play to her. She was invincible, omnipotent. In this frame of mind, she finally entered the building where the conference was to be held, and abruptly felt powerless, incompetent, and very vulnerable.

Somehow she managed to muddle through registration and being introduced to a woman named Frankie, who was putting her up for the night. It felt good to have someone she had an excuse to talk to, to find a table together at the coffee house that had been set up, and sit down to coffee and a sandwich.

"I'm sorry I don't have an extra bedroom, but there's lots of space in my apartment."

"That's fine," Emily reassured her. "I brought my sleeping bag." A couple of friends of Frankie's joined them at their table, and Frankie introduced Emily as her houseguest for the weekend.

"Oh, that's right," one of the women said to Frankie. "You're living alone again now, aren't you?" Was there some meaning attached to that, or to the way she glanced over at Emily as she said it?

"Yeah. I was telling her I have lots of *floor* space." Frankie turned again to Emily. "You can sleep in front of the fireplace if you like."

"I'd like that; it'll feel like home. W. . . I have a fireplace, too." She had almost ruined everything, denying herself all of those exciting women she could have been, and establishing her identity as only Sima's lover. Though she'd caught herself in time, it felt reckless, dangerous. What a lot of safety that one word could have provided.

The evening seemed very full. She was exhausted, and yet stimulated. It was amazing to be with so many other lesbians. She didn't have nerve enough to approach them or talk to any of them, but she watched them all, as she had been watching women her whole life, even when she was (was she really?) straight. She had always made up fantasies and stories about women she saw in crowds. Tonight, that wasn't happening.

Not that none of them were interesting. Sitting near her during the evening program was an enigmatic-looking woman with skin like polished walnut. Her hair was wrapped in a scarf of bright orange silk, and a jewel sparkled on the side of her nose. In front of Emily in the line for coffee, was a woman who couldn't be less than seventy, with white hair loose and abundant down her back, and patches all over her jeans. Frankie turned up again to talk during the break. Emily looked at her again, now, too—the mass of wiry, curly hair with its flashes of silver, the friendly face with its liberal sprinkling of freckles and, behind the rimless glasses, the eyes sincere brown. Her face was unique; Emily thought she was pretty. And yet, neither Frankie, nor any of the other women there, caught her fancy in the old way.

Instead, during the keynote address, she found her thoughts drifting to Sima. She pictured Sima sitting across from her at their kitchen table that morning, which now seemed like a week ago, pictured her drinking coffee from her yellow mug, brown hair in her eyes, eyes watching Emily over the cup. She remembered Sima's hug at the door of the bus. It would be two more days before she would hold her again.

The speaker was talking about monogamy. Emily's attention was caught. She had read one of the woman's books and liked it—a novel which did not seem at all critical of the monogamous relationship of its two main characters. Yet, the author was standing here before a roomful of women saying that she felt monogamy was outdated and didn't make sense for her life any more. Women who ended up in monogamous relationships, she said, were usually those who needed security most—the very security that monogamy prevented, the way it isolated those women from the community and forced them to depend only on each other.

So this was the other side of the question, the other point of view. Emily was surprised that it sounded so logical to her. At the same time, she felt annoyed with the author, kind of betrayed. What a disappointment that the two characters in that book might not have lived so happily ever after, after all.

That night, Frankie drove Emily out to her apartment on the north side. There had been other women in the car, but they had been dropped off, and now that she and Frankie were by themselves, Emily could think of nothing to say. She was aware that she was alone in a strange city with a woman she'd only just met, who was not even a friend of a friend, being driven to a destination she wouldn't recognize when they got there. What if. . . . She wasn't sure how that thought ended, glanced over at Frankie, who was silent now, too. She remembered something Sima had told her she'd read someplace—that often what you fear the most is really what you hope for.

She was relieved when they pulled up in front of an ordinary-looking apartment building. She was able to make conversation again as they carried her bags upstairs. Frankie showed her where things were, then left her to herself. Exhausted, Emily did not even take the time to write in her journal before going to sleep.

At the conference the following day, she chose to go to the session given by the novelist who had spoken the night before. She listened with interest as the woman spoke very frankly about her life, her lover, her work. When an opportunity came, Emily had a question. "Last night, when you were talking about monogamy and how you feel it doesn't work. . ." as the woman nodded, she went on, "I was wondering what alternatives you've found that do work."

"Actually," the author answered, smiling without a trace of apology, "none. I haven't found anything else that works either. Theoretically, the security could be provided by a supportive community. But in practice. . . ." Other women laughed know-ingly along with her, then broke into animated discussion. Emily was surprised that so many people had given this so much thought, pleased to hear those in favor of monogamy argue just as rationally and convincingly as those against it. From their illustrations, it seemed there were as many different ways to be monogamous as ways not to be.

But eventually, she grew tired of following the thread of the debate back and forth. Though she had listened to their voices, their thoughts, the women here were all still strangers. It was disappointing, but she realized now that that wasn't likely to change in the space of one weekend. She began to wonder what Sima would be saying if she were here—hoped she could re-member some of the points people had made, to tell her. It was Saturday, two o'clock. What would Sima be doing now? When the workshop broke up, she did not know which side had won the debate. What she remembered was looking at her watch again, and thinking that she was two hours closer to Sima.

When she and Frankie got back to the apartment that night, Frankie suggested they have a fire in the fireplace, since they had been too tired the night before. Emily offered to build it while Frankie made them cocoa. It was getting to be easy to talk to each other now. Over breakfast, Frankie had told Emily a lot about the women's community in Chicago, and in the car they had shared opinions on the day's workshops and the evening's performers. Now, Frankie had been telling Emily about last year's conference. Eventually she lapsed into silence, staring into the fire. When she spoke again, her voice was quieter. "It's really nice to have you stay here this weekend." She smiled at Emily, shaking her head a little. "You can't imagine how lonely it gets here, sometimes."

Emily felt the tension return, drawing her tight. She turned from the fire to glance across at the figure seated near her. Frankie seemed as attractive as she had before—leaning back now, relaxed, against the bottom of the couch, one leg bent and the other stretched out. Emily watched while she lit a cigarette almost too slowly, watched her fingers flick the burning match into the fire. Then those earnest brown eyes were turned back on her, and she realized she should answer with something.

"I've been feeling lonely this weekend, too." Now why had she said that? What would be the response?

Was it real, or did she only imagine a hopefulness in the questioning look Frankie gave her, an interest in her voice as she asked, "You have?"

It flashed in Emily's mind that this was the chance she had longed for—to find out what it might be like if she wasn't Sima's lover. That chance was presented so quickly, either to be plunged into immediately or passed up forever, with no guarantee—no assurance that Frankie's thoughts were anything like her own. She looked back into the fire, then turned again to that face full of friendly curiosity under the crop of wiry curls. "Yes," she finally answered. Took a deep breath and went on. "I miss my lover: Sima."

Frankie's face broke into a smile. "A weekend can be a long time when you're in love."

Emily smiled, too. The moment was past. She could feel the muscles in her shoulders relaxing, and the sigh that escaped her was one of relief. Maybe that chance had never really existed; maybe nothing had been there but her own imagination getting carried away, and a sympathetic woman in this unfamiliar city, trying to make a stranger feel like a friend.

After Frankie had said good night, Emily stayed up watching the fire, remembering a night last winter, when she and Sima had built a fire. She could see Sima in her perennial pullover sweater and corduroy jeans, squatting before the fire, fanning the flames with a fold of newspaper, could see Sima's face turned toward her, warm and bright and glowing with the reflection of the firelight, the brown eyes laughing. She had run to put her arms around Sima, gather her all in and hug her tight, and they had laughed and begun to make love. Maybe tomorrow night, something like that. . . .

The last day of the conference was devoted entirely to an open reading. Though she was anxious to get home, Emily wanted to take this chance to read her work to other lesbians, something she had never done. She had read in public only as a "woman poet" in a male-dominated literary community, trying to write according to their standards, meet their criticism. Her work was different, now, and she had to know how it would be taken by this group.

The women took turns standing in the opening of the circle of chairs to read. As she listened, Emily grew more and more impressed with their work. They were good readers. They were able to project their voices, make the music of their words come alive, keep the audience hanging on every line. She knew she could read well, too, if fear did not get the better of her.

She tried to concentrate on the poet who was beginning to read now. Then she noticed that in the chair next to the one just vacated, sat a woman who was a clump of tension and anxiety, even more nervous than the one who was reading. Emily knew in an instant that she was the reader's lover. Would Sima be afraid and nervous like that? She wouldn't want to put Sima through that, but how she wished for her here, now, to lean over and whisper that her poetry was as good as any of this stuff. There was no one in this audience who knew her, no one to squeeze her hand when her turn came, or be waiting to hug her when she came back to her seat.

It was time. She stood up and walked to the opening in the circle. The poems were about Sima and herself, about loving

each other. At the end of the first one, she could not tell how
well she'd done, was shocked by the solidness of the applause.
She felt safe, now. It was easy to read the others. And the audience loved them. They laughed outright at the lines that were
meant to be funny, clapped long and loud at the end. In the
break that followed, Frankie came to hug her. And a circle of
other women stood near to tell her that they liked what she'd
read. The novelist caught her near the door to say she felt Emily's
was some of the best lesbian poetry she'd ever heard. And
suddenly Emily realized she felt as if there were friends there,
a lot of friends to say good-bye to, before she finally left to catch
the subway, then the bus for O'Hare field again.

She had not come right out and asked to be met at the airport,
but she had hinted around, making sure that Sima knew the
flight number and arrival time. So she was a little disappointed
when no one was there to meet her flight. She was much more
disappointed when the apartment door did not open in answer
to her ringing their special signal of the bell. Using her key to
enter the apartment, she found the rooms clean and orderly,
but empty. In the kitchen, at her place at the table, was an
envelope addressed to her in Sima's hand.

Emily hung her coat on a chair back and set down her things
on the kitchen floor, sat down to open the letter.

> Sunday morning
>
> Emmy, love,
>
> I have thought a lot while you've been away,
> about us, and about you and the reasons you
> went to the conference. I know you take your
> writing seriously and I respect you as a writer.
> But I can't help feeling there was more to it
> than that.
>
> For some time now, I've felt you growing dis-
> tant from me. I know you tell me you love me
> and I want to believe it, and try to, but some-
> times it's hard. I know I have a jealous nature,
> and maybe I'm over-possessive, but it feels like
> you're not happy with me any more, like my
> love is not enough for you and you want to move
> on to something newer and more exciting.
>
> It used to be, that whenever we had to go

through something scary, we always talked about it and told each other our fears. I kept hoping you'd want to do that before you left. When you didn't, I couldn't bring myself to tell you mine. But I will now. I was afraid that you went to Chicago hoping you'd meet someone there that you could love more than me. And now I'm afraid that you have.

I've thought about this a whole lot, and it feels like all the signs were there. I've been pretty unhappy all weekend, but I guess I've accepted it now.

If you really want to leave, please do it tonight, and we can talk about it and work out the details tomorrow or another day. There's some extra money in the tin, if you need it for tonight. I know your flight comes in at six, and I want to give you lots of time, so I won't be home till around twelve or one.

Maybe we don't have to end what we have this way. But if that's what you want, I want you to feel free to make that choice. And if we do decide to stay together, let's make that a conscious choice, too. I still love you.

                                        Sima

Emily hadn't slept much all weekend, but hours later she was still wide awake, with every light in the house burning. It was after one-thirty a.m. when she heard the outside door. No special rings, just the key in the lock and then the door swinging shut with that familiar bang. She flung open the door to the corridor. In the bright light of the hallway, every detail was clear—Sima's brown hair disheveled and windblown, her eyes, as she lifted them, puffy and red. Amazement, then relief flooded her face. There was only a fraction of a second for Emily to take all that in, and they were in each other's arms.

A long time passed before either of them could talk. It was Sima who said it first. "I'm sorry. I feel awful."

"You're not the only one." Very soon—tomorrow, maybe even tonight—she knew she would tell Sima everything, right from the beginning. . . .

Sima sighed and drew back to meet Emily's eyes again. This time, her face held the beginnings of a sheepish smile. "One thing I know," she said softly. "It'll be a lot easier. . .next time."

SAFEKEEPING

The ring had a brown stone mounted on a wide band the color of silver. The band was worn shiny, ice-thin and sharp as a slice. She had cut herself on it, once. In the center of the band, the flat oval stone had been surrounded by a zig-zag border of tiny triangles, but now they were worn away, and even the cloudy face of the stone was chipped at its edges. Bronwyn had worn the ring for seven years. Everything that had happened in those years, she had told to Roseanne.

It had been easy to tell things to Roseanne, then. They had been friends, Roseanne and Bronwyn, seated so often at opposite ends of the little couch, facing, with feet tucked up underneath, telling out stories of all the years of their lives. Between them, they had fifty years of stories to tell. And it was the telling that made things become so special between them.

With Roseanne, it had seemed easy, Bronwyn remembered, to talk about the men who had stumbled into and out of her life, to tell of the many who had known her intimately, the ones she had loved, the way they had not loved her—to talk about rejections, and aloneness, and pain.

One of those stories, a little different from so many of the others, was the story of the ring. The ring had belonged, she told Roseanne, to a man whose name was Ira. It was seven years, now, since he and Bronwyn had befriended each other. Seven years ago, they were both too young to be lovers, and Bronwyn thought it was better that way because it was pure, because it was spiritual. So they had been friends who might have been lovers, if they had not been young enough to be too wise for that. They were friends who could love each other, and tell each other so. With Ira, Bronwyn felt completely safe. They spent one summer together. It was long enough to choose, between them, the values by which they intended to live the rest of their lives.

At the end of that summer, when it was time to leave each other, Ira had taken off the ring with the brown stone and given it to her. She had given him her ring, too—a fragile thing of silver wire that she had bought at a carnival, which only fit on his smallest finger. Neither of them could have said, then, why she would wear his ring for all these years, or why he had worn hers.

He had worn Bronwyn's ring until the night he went to a party and met the woman he would marry. The woman had admired Bronwyn's silver wire ring, and he had let her hold it and try it on, then replaced it upon his own finger. He had not thought about it again, but when he got home from the party, he realized it was gone. Ira searched for it, and the woman he'd met searched, and the people who gave the party searched their home, with no success. He wrote to Bronwyn to apologize. He wrote to her, a few months later, to announce his engagement.

Bronwyn had once met a sorceress, a witch, a woman of magic. She had taken Bronwyn's hand in hers and studied the ring with the brown stone. She told Bronwyn that it was a magic ring, heavy with power, that it was very old and had been worn on many hands. The sorceress said she knew that the ring was not Bronwyn's, but had been given into her keeping by someone else. She said that, like all rings, all stones, the ring gave Bronwyn special power over the person to whom it belonged. She would not disclose what that power was.

After that, Bronwyn liked to finger the ring, to turn it round and round where it fit loose on her largest finger, and think about Ira, and what the power that she held over him might be. Sometimes she thought that the ring would bring them back together, and would create between them what they had been too young, or too wise to seek from each other before. Sometimes she thought the power of the ring kept him apart from her. If she deliberately removed the ring, what protection, or burden would Ira be free of? Or was it really herself that the power of the ring controlled? She thought about her own little silver ring and how, the same night that Ira had lost it, he had found the woman who married him. Bronwyn had attended their wedding where she had embraced the other woman. She had cried at the wedding, and left it feeling that she had truly given him away. She wondered if she might lose Ira's ring some day, too. But, though it was so large on her finger, she did not lose it, and for all these years she had not removed it.

That was what Bronwyn told, when Roseanne asked her about the ring. And it was easy to tell it, then, because at that time they were only friends.

As time passed, Roseanne became her confidante, and her closest friend. Roseanne became her compañera, became kindred. Nights of telling each other stories, they drew closer now; they began to touch one another with more than words. And a new time began.

Roseanne became Bronwyn's source of delight, her secret, her star-wish. Roseanne became her lover. And on the night that they became lovers, Bronwyn removed the ring. It was suddenly too heavy, too obtrusive. It did not belong on the hand she wanted empty and gentle to love Roseanne. The following morning, the ring lay on the polished surface of the night table. As Bronwyn studied it in the morning light, it looked very worn, very old. She wrapped it in a clean handkerchief and slipped it into a corner of the drawer. She knew she would not wear it again.

For the first time in many seasons, Bronwyn received a letter from Ira. It came to the house where she now lived with Roseanne, for even though Bronwyn and Ira had not seen each other since his wedding long ago, and seldom wrote, they had always let each other know where they were living. In this letter, he told of the breaking up of his marriage. The news was disturbing to Bronwyn. She had imagined that Ira was happy. But he was alone again and seeking her as a friend; she was uncertain how that friendship would fit into her life with Roseanne. She wrote him an answer, telling of Roseanne's and her love.

In his next letter, Ira said he would come to visit. He would come for just one day from the city two hundred miles away, where he lived now. He wanted to see her, to talk to her.

Bronwyn was apprehensive. As she grew in her love with Roseanne, she had grown cautious of all men, more cautious still of men from her own past. It had happened before, that

men who had refused to return her love years ago, at a time
when she wanted them to, had reappeared, trying to impose
themselves on her, now, when she had no use for them, when
there was all the love she could ever want from Roseanne. Such
men would try to change her, to change Roseanne; when they
left, they were not friends any more. Maybe Ira would be like
that, too, though he had never refused her his love in the past—
for what it was worth, he had said. And he had never imposed
his presence on her—but he had been very young, then; perhaps
he had grown to be like the others.

Ira entered the house and Bronwyn knew instantly that he
had not changed. He brought no threat, no danger with him—
there was still that soft safeness that she had first begun to
love him for. He was the friend she remembered; he would be
Roseanne's friend now, too. But his face was changed—awak-
ened—alive and radiant.

Ira listened, intent, while she told him of the changes in her
life. He questioned her, wanted to know the entire sequence, all
that she wanted to tell. When she reached her ending, he told
her that he was happy for her, took her hand. He did not ask
about the missing ring. Surely he understood why she so longer
wore it. He had something else to talk of, now.

Bronwyn—he said—I have something to tell you. I have fallen
in love, too. His name is David.

She had known it, had known what he would say. It felt as if
she'd known this—what they were both just finding out about
each other, about themselves—for a long time. Perhaps she
had even known as far back as that summer long ago, when
they had been wise enough to choose each other for friends.

A FOUR SIDED FIGURE

In the last box were things that neither of them was quite sure what to do with. Things that seemed to stubbornly retain the identity of belonging to one woman or the other, to resist becoming part of "ours" as the two put together this new home for both of them: a pair of pillows that was extra now with only one bed; the curtain of wooden beads that had hung in the entryway of Kelcy's old apartment and made it so hard for Ellen to slip in and surprise her, even with her own key; Ellen's small braided rugs that there was no need for with Kelcy's room-sized Persian carpets. And there was the decoupage.

It was a small square piece of old but polished wood, with a picture applied to it in the soft, muted tones of that art form, a picture of two women—kissing.

As she ran her fingers over the smooth wood of the beads and pretended to be considering where they might hang them in this new apartment, Ellen saw its corner sticking up. She remembered it clearly from the time she had first known Kelcy, when it had hung above the couch in her living room. She had liked it immediately, gone closer to admire it, and then drawn back as she saw the initials, J.M., in the corner, heard Kelcy's unnecessary explanation—yes, it was done by Jamie, her former lover. In time, it had disappeared from that wall, along with the enlarged photographs and the oil portrait of Kelcy and Jamie together. She knew that the photographs and the portrait had been given to Jamie, but apparently this small wooden plaque had not.

As if reading her thoughts, Kelcy pulled it out of the box and said, "I guess I won't hang this up here...."

"Oh, yes." Ellen took the thing from Kelcy's hands, the hands she loved to watch kneading bread, watering plants, writing letters—loved to watch them and think about them making love to her. She looked at Kelcy's hands now as she said, "You can hang it up here. I don't mind; I think it's pretty."

"Are you sure?" Kelcy took it back, a doubtful look in her dark eyes as she turned them toward Ellen. "You know that Jamie. . . ."

"I know," Ellen interrupted her. "I know about you and Jamie." She was still getting used to it, though. It was so different from her own life, in which there had been no one before Kelcy. She shrugged. "I can't pretend you never had a past, never loved anyone but me."

Kelcy responded with a sudden quick hug and kiss. "I do love you," she said.

They chose a spot on the wall over the small oak dresser that had been Ellen's before. She watched while Kelcy handled the hammer, watched her competent hands at their task. And for the first time, it occurred to her that those same small hands had also made love with Jamie—not once, but many times.

As she came in from work, Ellen surveyed the apartment with pleasure as she always did. In only a few weeks it had lost its cluttered, transitional look, and become the home she had always dreamed of. In the bedroom, while she stripped off her skirt and nylons, she let her eyes travel over all the items she loved. The things which had been hers, which had journeyed with her through apartments and communal houses, and the things she would never have thought of owning, but which she loved simply because they were Kelcy's. The patchwork afghan that Kelcy had crocheted, draped across the rocking chair, or the ornate camel-saddle footstool—these things seemed as rare and exotic as Kelcy herself.

As she opened the dresser drawer for a pair of socks, her eye was caught by the decoupage. Perhaps it was good she had agreed to hang it up. She'd grown to like it more; it somehow made her feel safe. As if Kelcy's past was out in the open like everything else between them, and therefore could not hurt her.

When Kelcy came in, Ellen noticed that she seemed distracted, distant. The hug they shared did not seem to relieve her tension tonight, nor did her relating all the little annoyances and irritations of her day at work. Later, as they lingered at the table after dinner, Kelcy said suddenly, "Jamie called me at work today."

Ellen felt the tension charge through her body like electricity. She avoided Kelcy's eyes, spooning another sugar into her coffee, but her voice sounded off key as she answered, "Yeah?"

"Oh, it's nothing bad." Their eyes met, and she knew that Kelcy, too, was thinking of other times Jamie had called. Times when Jamie had been depressed and felt, still, she had no one to turn to but Kelcy, even though it was supposed to be over between them. Times when Jamie had tried to convince Kelcy it was all a mistake, to beg her to break up with Ellen and come back to her. Times when a five minute phone call had caused a whole evening of pain.

"No," Kelcy was saying. "In fact, it's kind of good. She said she's met another woman that she likes and she's feeling a whole lot happier."

Relief flooded Ellen's body as she said, "That's wonderful. I'm really glad."

"And she says," Kelcy looked away for a second, then back, "she says she'd like us to come over for dinner one night this week. She wants us to meet her friend and she wants to meet you. I think she feels better now that she's found someone, too. More like she can accept the fact that you're for real in my life.

"I'd kind of like to go," she went on. "I haven't seen her since I gave her back those pictures and," she looked wistful, like a little girl wanting something very much, "I do care what happens to her, even though I'm not in love with her any more. Maybe we could be friends with them."

Ellen hesitated, playing with her teaspoon, then looked up to meet those dark eyes full of question. How could she say no to anything when Kelcy looked like that? "It's o.k.," she said slowly. "It might be good for me to meet Jamie—I mean she *was* important to you. Maybe trying to avoid her would be making it into a bigger thing than it is. It is a little...scary, but we can go."

"Don't worry." Kelcy smiled and reached across the table to take her hand. "I really mean it when I say I'm not in love with her any more. I don't want to go chasing after her or change my mind. I've made up my mind I want to be with you."

Kelcy made the call and arranged for dinner at six the day after next. Once it was done, they both felt lighthearted and relieved. Ellen forgot about Jamie and they played records and danced together all evening, then read each other to sleep.

But in the following two days, she thought about Jamie more. She recalled Jamie's image from the pictures and tried to imagine her and Kelcy together, found herself wondering what it was like when they broke up. Pictured Kelcy angry—tossing her hair back the way she did, the dark light flashing in her eyes and that closed, tough look that masked her rage. Yet Ellen would know that inside she was as hurt and vulnerable as a wounded wild creature. Had Jamie seen that, too? Or had she just gone on cruelly hurting? When Ellen imagined those scenes, she wished she could have been there to come between the two and protect Kelcy.

Jamie was beginning to take on the dimensions of a romantic figure, a character from a story or a movie. Kelcy seemed always a little like that.

In spite of all her speculations, Ellen was not prepared when Jamie opened the door of her apartment that night. She had pictured brown hair, and longer. Really it was auburn—almost red, cut short now, and curly. She'd pictured her the wrong size; Jamie was no bigger than Kelcy—the same slight figure, small proportioned. She was dressed, too, in the same style Kelcy wore—faded denims, turtleneck, flannel shirt. Ellen found herself wondering if they had worn each other's clothes, something she and Kelcy could not do. She had to admit that Jamie's face, with its scattering of freckles across the snub nose, was appealing. And yet, when that face was turned to greet Ellen, the smile, which had seemed real enough for Kelcy, was no longer convincing.

She had not given a thought to the other woman, but now Jamie introduced her as Mocha. She was tall and slender, with a cocoa brown complexion and black hair in a soft, full afro. She did not smile at Kelcy as she said hello, but looked relieved to meet Ellen. This must be just as hard for her, Ellen thought, and she felt an instant kinship. They were sisters in this venture.

All of them were on guard. Each handled it differently. Mocha sat like a dancer, body held in, the few motions spare and controlled. Her eyes were cautious, suspicious. She's afraid of losing her lover, Ellen decided. For Mocha was watching Jamie, as if just waiting for the word or gesture that she would pounce on as betrayal.

Now Ellen watched Jamie, too. She seemed to be trying to act as if the four of them were just two couples who were getting together as old friends. She was overdoing it, full of witty conversation, jokes, and long dramatic anecdotes. The whole thing appeared to be directed at Kelcy, but her eyes, when they did glance Ellen's way, seemed to smoulder. I'm still some kind of intruder, Ellen thought, some detour in the way she thinks Kelcy's life is supposed to go. It began to annoy her, Jamie's endless stories, the clear, compelling quality of her voice, her frequent laugh as she tilted back her curly head.

It annoyed her, too, that Kelcy seemed to be enjoying it fine, that she appeared so comfortable, so much at ease, so confident. Ellen took in the fluid posture, the shining cascade of rich dark hair, the small hands that were her own weakness, clasped together around one knee. Any woman might feel jealous about a lover, with Kelcy around to look at. She couldn't blame Mocha. She almost couldn't blame Jamie.

But she couldn't get past a feeling of danger, mistrust. Was it only Jamie she didn't trust? How was it that Kelcy could appear so relaxed? What was she so confident of?

Her attention had travelled round the circuit of the small square figure formed by the four of them seated facing on the floor, to end at herself. How did she appear to the others? She couldn't sit still, her clothes felt rumpled and tacky, and she had hardly said a word since she came in. She shifted uneasily and tried to pay attention to the conversation.

Jamie had continued to fill in the time with stories that they were all able to laugh at, if only to relieve some of the tension. It was after one of those ridiculous stories that Kelcy turned to Mocha, laughing still, and said, cocking her head toward Jamie, "Where did you pick her up, anyway?" They all laughed for real, then, and seconds later the bell on the oven timer sounded for dinner. It was easier after that.

Walking home, she was still sorting out her feelings when Kelcy asked her how the evening had been for her. "It was o.k."

"But...?" Kelcy prompted. She touched Ellen's arm, but Ellen kept her fists shoved deep in her pockets. "You didn't have a good time, did you? I'm sorry. ..."

Kelcy looked so crestfallen that Ellen found herself relenting. "It's not your fault. I'm just not very good at this yet—coming face to face with your past. I can't help...wondering...."

"Wondering what?"

"I don't know. Just wondering. The same kind of thing Jamie probably wonders."

"And what's that?" Kelcy asked gently.

They walked on silently for half a block before Ellen answered. "She wants to know if you love me more than her. And I want to know if you love...loved her more than you love me."

"Ellen, don't. It's different, being with you. You know I love you a whole lot, and I *have* chosen to be with you and not with her any more. But I don't want to make comparisons. It's just different."

"I know. I'm not asking you to answer the question." But inside, she was disappointed. She was glad Kelcy had not asked what she thought of Mocha and Jamie. She liked Mocha—could empathize with her caution and guardedness. And she liked the way Mocha had not really gone along with Jamie's social game. But she knew she didn't like Jamie. And felt irritated that there had been no way she could gracefully object when Kelcy had suggested that Jamie and Mocha return the visit next week.

In the days that preceded that visit, she tried not to think about it—but Jamie kept showing up in her thoughts at the oddest moments. Like on Sunday, when she watched Kelcy sifting together the flour and beating the eggs to make bread. Ellen surprised herself by asking, "Where did you get the bread recipe you use?"

"From Jamie," came the inevitable answer. "She taught me how to bake bread."

Ellen was silent. Even though she had known Kelcy would say that, she felt angry. And when the bread was done and they ate hot buttery slices fresh from the oven, it didn't taste quite as good as usual, and she refused a second piece.

She also found herself looking at Kelcy's things with a new eye. For instance, her jewelry. She had a lot of pretty earrings and bracelets but Ellen had never, in all the time she had known Kelcy, seen her buy a piece of jewelry. Now she studied the bright rings and bangles jumbled in the velvet lined box and wondered. Were all of these, possibly, gifts from Jamie?

As Ellen set the table for breakfast, she looked at Kelcy's patterned dishes and thought that she and Jamie must have chosen the pattern together. She put those dishes back on the shelf and set the table with her own mismatched china. Things that she had previously loved because they were Kelcy's, she now began to dislike because they were once Jamie's, too.

Even in bed with Kelcy, it occurred to her that the two of them must have slept together under the very same blue corduroy comforter. She couldn't help thinking about it while they were making love. Had they done the same things? Had Jamie been more aggressive than she was? More receptive? Had Kelcy liked it better making love with Jamie?

She awaited the coming Saturday night with mixed feelings. She felt a kind of dreadful fascination with Jamie, a curiosity that wanted to know her thoroughly, wanted her to cease to be a mystery. At the same time, she was afraid of more contact with her, found herself wishing the weekend would never come.

From the first hour that Saturday morning, things seemed to go wrong. Waking early, she slipped out of bed, showered, and got dressed before Kelcy awoke. That was not their usual pattern on Saturdays, which was frequently a day on which they made love, or just lay close touching and talking for an hour or so before attacking the day. As she tiptoed through the bedroom on her way from the bathroom, she saw that Kelcy was awake and could tell, by the look in her eyes, that she was hurt and disappointed. Kelcy beckoned to her and drew her close to kiss her, and she could feel the urging invitation in her touch; she knew Kelcy could feel the resistance in her own. With a sigh, Kelcy, too, got up and started to dress.

In the supermarket, they began to disagree over brands of food, a thing they had not done since they first bought food together. Kelcy upheld that the ingredients in all brands of margerine were the same, regulated by law, while Ellen insisted that she could taste the difference, even if Kelcy could not. They compromised, but too late not to feel the discomfort linger between them, and Ellen wondered why it mattered so much today when before, she would eat anything she thought Kelcy liked.

As Kelcy collected clothes to take to the laundromat, they quarrelled again. "Where's your purple shirt with the long sleeves, the Indian print one you like so much?"

Ellen answered absently, searching under the sink for detergent and fabric softener. "I don't know, but it's not important. You can just take whatever of mine's in the basket."

"Oh." A pause, then, "I thought you might want to wear it tonight."

"What for?" She could hear her own voice grow sharper. "Just because Jamie and Mocha are coming for dinner? I don't need to try to make an impression on *them*."

"I didn't say that. But. . . ."

"But?"

"Well, I thought you felt like it was kind of special. We've never had people over for dinner and. . . ."

"And I'm not getting dressed up for it. I *hate* getting dressed up. And I don't see any reason for you to get dressed up either."

Kelcy only said, "I always thought you *liked* that shirt." But she left the house without giving Ellen a good-bye hug.

After Kelcy was gone, Ellen was annoyed at herself. She had been feeling mean and irritable all day, but she needn't have quarrelled over something so insignificant. She *did* like the purple shirt.

Alone in the apartment, she wandered through its rooms deep in thought. In the bedroom, the four sided wooden decoration caught her eye. She stared at the picture, searching its colors and lines. Two women in an embrace, a kiss. Their faces partly obscured by their hair—one's straight and dark, the other's curlier, shorter, almost red. It was suddenly clear who they were. She gently lifted the ornament from the wall and turned it over in her hands. Beneath the picture wire, on the back, words were engraved in the dark wood. "From Jamie to Kelcy. Happy 5th Anniversary. I'll always love you." She turned it back over, then carefully replaced it where it had been.

When Kelcy came in, Ellen found it easy to stay out of her way. She worked in the living room—dusting, putting albums away in their jackets, vacuuming the carpet—while Kelcy put away the laundry and began making dinner. She knew Kelcy would expect her in the kitchen to make the salad, but it was only when she could find absolutely nothing else to clean in the rest of the apartment that she reluctantly made her way to the kitchen.

She stopped short in the doorway. There was no mistaking the fragrant aroma from the pot on the stove. Kelcy was making sauce. Ellen walked to the stove and lifted the lid, and was met by the rich, spicy tomato smell. She was sure she remembered a scrap of a long forgotten conversation... "Isn't that Jamie's favorite food—spaghetti?" Kelcy nodded, her black eyes apprehensive, as Ellen abruptly turned away.

In the bedroom, she stared out the window while she heard Kelcy follow her across the room to within a few feet. She felt immobile, her muscles stiff, as Kelcy asked, "Is it that important?"

"Yes! No, not just that." She turned to face Kelcy. "Lately, it seems like our lives have started to revolve around Jamie."

"Jamie! Is that what's been bothering you? Since when?"

"Ever since we started this whole escapade—everything that's happened."

"Like what?"

Ellen groped for an illustration. Her eyes, quickly scanning the room, fastened on the decoupage, and she went to remove it from the wall. "Like this." She thrust it into Kelcy's hands. "Why didn't you tell me? I thought it was just supposed to be a picture of two women. And why didn't you tell me what it says on the back?"

Kelcy bent over it as if examining it for the first time. Finally she said, "Oh, Ellen. I thought you knew. I thought, when you said to hang it up, you must have really looked at it, looked at the other side, and that you must know."

Ellen drew back widely to stare at Kelcy. "Must know? Know what?" Her fears raced far ahead of her words. "Tell me, Kelcy. What am I supposed to know?"

Kelcy looked again at the object she held, licked her lips, and Ellen felt herself going tight with fear. "What it meant to me ..." the answer came slowly. "This—" she indicated the decoupage, "—and my relationship with Jamie. What the past means to me. I didn't know that was what was bothering you. And I don't want it to make you feel bad. But it was eight years of my life. I can't just forget it, obliterate it, act like it never happened. Even if I wanted to."

"But you don't want to."

Slowly Kelcy shook her head. "No. It wasn't all bad. We didn't always fight the way we did at the end. We were happy." Ellen's face was burning, her throat full of tears. She turned back to the window. Kelcy's voice was right behind her. "Ellen, I'm not saying these things to try to hurt you. You know it's over now. Jamie knows it, too. I can tell her again tonight, if it'll make you feel better. I just don't want to hide anything from you. And I didn't want to have to deny my past. I was hoping you could accept it all." She put her hands softly on Ellen's shoulders, but Ellen turned swiftly, displacing them.

"And what if I can't?"

Kelcy looked down at the square of wood, where it lay on the dresser. With a finger, she traced the lines of the letters engraved in the wood. Her voice, when she answered, was almost inaudible. "Then I'll change. I'll throw this out. And we won't be friends with Jamie and Mocha. I'll call them up and tell them I'm sick, or you're sick—oh, hell, I'll tell them the truth. Ellen, you're more important to me than all of that. I guess that's what I thought you knew."

Ellen was crying again. This time, she didn't pull away, but let Kelcy enfold her in her arms. . . .

The jangle of the doorbell startled them both. They pulled apart in dismay.

"I'll get it." Kelcy stood up. "I'll just go down and tell them —"

"Wait!" Then Ellen hesitated while Kelcy looked at her curiously. How could she explain to Kelcy what was not even clear to herself, why she wanted what she did: to go on with this thing now, whether it drew the two couples close to each other or drove them apart—to go through it, and beyond it. She could not find the words quickly for an explanation. The passing seconds seemed to press against them like water against a thin barrier. She said, "I think we should go through with it."

Kelcy shook her head decidedly. "We don't have to."

"I know. I want us to." The words hung in the air between

them, sounding almost defiant, a challenge. She realized she had been holding her breath when she saw the decisiveness yielding in Kelcy's face, heard her answer.

"Are you sure it's o.k.?"

"As long as we're in it together...."

The bell sounded again, longer, more insistent. Ellen strode into the next room to push the buzzer that opened the downstairs door.

She stood in the open doorway, hearing the heavy foyer door bang shut. A second later, she felt Kelcy come up behind her and put her arms around her. They held still, waiting, listening to the footsteps on the uncarpeted treads, to the two voices rising from four flights down.

FOR NIGHTS LIKE THIS ONE

The first of those dreams had been years ago. At that time when Covey had expected changes in her life to come from someone outside herself, when she had still expected something of men and had sometimes slept with one of them rather than be by herself. But the night of the dream, she had gone to sleep alone. And dreamt that she awoke to find her old friend, Dierdre, lying beside her under the blue wool blanket. Dierdre was crying. Covey, in the center of the dream, felt confused and helpless to make Dierdre feel better, wanting to put her arms around her but afraid. Using words instead, saying, "Don't cry, Dierdre. It's all right. Please don't cry." Finally reaching to touch her and instead waking in a sudden start.

Lying awake, she felt confused still, disturbed by her reaction. She could feel her heart beating at twice the pace of sleep, and her body was hot all over, like a fever. She relived the fragment of dream, remembering Dierdre beside her—face buried in her arms in the pillow so that only the black curls were visible, her shoulders shaking with sobs under the soft blue wool. Awake, Covey wondered—what would have happened if I had touched her, if I had put my arms around her? And did not understand why the dream seemed so highly charged with feeling, with portent.

There were similar dreams after that, first a few, then many, recurring with increasing frequency. The woman in the dream was not always the same. Sometimes she began as someone Covey had known, like Dierdre or another friend, or one of her sisters. Sometimes the dream woman would be all of them, merging through different women that Covey had been close to easily, illusively. More often, she would be no one Covey knew. Or it would not be clear *who* she was—the face, features, figures indistinct and vague. What would be distinct were the sensations Covey felt—the excitement as the woman appeared in any dream, the anticipation. Then the woman might approach her and in the dream (or through the dream) Covey would feel a rising rush of excitement. There was never much between them physically in the dreams. Not much had to happen—just brushing close, or taking hands was enough to send Covey through to the other side of the sensations. It would happen quickly, and yet she would feel complete emotional and physical satisfaction.

She would usually wake, then, and think about the dream as she lay awake in the night. Wondering why it was so easy in the dreams, easy to approach so close to someone else, not to be afraid, not to be self-conscious. Wondering why it was so easy in the dreams, also, to reach the place she always wanted to reach, that warm, sensual flush of fulfillment that was so rare for her in real life. When she was alone with herself, it was sometimes attainable, but it was never easy—always had to be cultivated and nurtured, brought carefully to blossom. Outside herself, her physical experiences had been with men. Now she no longer allowed them that close. Their disappointing attempts at affection had finally convinced her that they did not know anything at all of the place she wanted to reach. Yet that place could be arrived at so easily, so naturally, with the women—or woman in the dreams.

Covey preferred to think of her as one woman—not the number of women she appeared to be, but one, capable of all those transmutations. The woman began to be a part of her waking dreams as well as the night dreams. In the· daytime, Covey was often lonely, and she decided to be open to this woman from her own subconscious, to let her into her life and allow her to be a companion, a confidante, a friend. She named her Skye.

Now when she was lonely, when her house seemed too large and empty for her alone, it was Skye she conjured up to be there with her. Wherever there was warmth—it was Skye.

Covey's two hands closing around the warmth of her coffee
mug, and she'd close her eyes and feel the warmth of Skye's
hand instead. In the morning, in the shower, Covey'd let the hot
water stream down her back, savoring the warmth and the
soft hard touches in a hundred places at once on her skin. That
was Skye again, laughing in the shower with her, and the
shower-warmth was being hugged. Before going to bed at night,
Covey would pile a heap of blankets on the bed, tucking them
tight at the sides, not only because the house grew cold at night,
but because she loved the weight of them, loved to slide between
their tight hold that now became Skye's hold. And at night
there was always the chance that Skye would be there in a
dream.

Sometimes she would talk to Skye. Mostly say the things that
seemed missing, that seemed to need to be said in the emptiness
she fought against in her life. "You don't ever have to be unhappy again. You'll never have to be alone again. I'm going to
be here with you. I'm going to stay with you and love you. You'll
always be loved."

She liked to imagine Skye saying those kinds of things to her.
And other things, too. About Covey. Skye would like Covey's
body. She would be able to talk about that and tell Covey the
things she liked. "I like the colors,"she would say. "All the
different shades of brown melting together. Like mixing up
gingerbread or spice cake—the ginger, cinnamon, nutmeg,
allspice, all running together. Gingercake."

Or another time, "You're like the country, like the land out in
New Mexico. Pueblo country, mesas and clay, full of earthiness
and simplicity. The beauty is very subtle but exquisite. You
have to be from that kind of country to be able to see it all, to be
able to love it."

She would like Covey's hair, like to comb it out with the
tortoise-shell pik while it was still wet and tangle-free, the
drops shining like crystals. When it was dry, she would like to
catch her fingers in it, or trace the rough ruffled shape of it
with her hands. "Like a thundercloud," she'd say. "An angry
little thundercloud." And she would make Covey laugh and like
it, too.

Skye would like the shape of Covey. The roundness and full-
ness would fit in the curve of her hands, and fill her arms. Skye

would like the touch of her—the places that were smooth and tender, and those that were hard or rough, scarred or calloused. Would finger those places on Covey's hands and knees and feet very gently, and sometimes she would kiss them.

Covey knew she was in love with Skye, and she knew why— she wanted to love a woman. In Covey's dreams and fantasies, Skye had been created of many women. It was possible that, in the real world as well, there were many women who could be Skye. Covey began to search for them—for her. Wherever there were many people she searched for Skye. She looked for her at the groceries and markets, and began to enjoy shopping. She watched all the passersby out the windows of the laundromat or shoe repair—any place she had to wait. She no longer minded the clinic, the food stamp office—those places were full of women. On the bus each day she examined every one carefully.

Sometimes she would catch a glimpse of Skye. Although Skye's image was not clear in her mind, she'd recognize bits and pieces of it, at times. She'd hear a voice that, while not even addressing her, seemed to be caressing her, rough and soft at the same time, like the feel of a cat's tongue—Skye's voice. Or she'd be caught by a pair of eyes that were as deep and compelling as a flame. She'd see Skye's hands, or her walk, or hear her laugh.

It began to change things for her, this search for Skye. Covey, who used always to be alone, to be at home, who had chosen to live by herself—began to want to be with other people as often as she could. With women. She became aware of these other women now, apart from her search for Skye. Sometimes, when she looked at a back, or a face, or a figure across the street, she'd find herself looking again, even when she knew the other woman could not be Skye. And going to places where women were likely to be, watching them, taking them in, grew to be satisfying in themselves.

There was a woman who began to work at a place where Covey worked, who Covey found herself watching in that way. A woman with black eyes and black hair, and skin the color of wet sand on the shore.

What was appealing was the contrasts, the way this woman could be two different ways at once. That a part of her was so traditionally feminine—lace on her sleeves, a bit of embroidery showing under the bib of her overalls. Or a gesture—her hand brushing back a strand of hair that had escaped being caught in the two practical braids. At the same time, she would not be feminine at all, but tough and taut and resilient, as acid as she was sweet. She'd swear outrageously at an empty box that tumbled down from where she'd shoved it. In one leap, she'd clear the space from the ground to the open back of the delivery truck, and lift sacks weighing fifty pounds as easily as if she were lifting a child.

Appealing, too, was the way she moved as she worked, her strength flowing as easily and as naturally as her grace. Once Covey watched her stand on a ladder and stretch to the top of her height to fit a heavy box into a space above. Watched the lovely long line her body made reaching, head tilted back, the sweep from her chin down her throat, and the profile of her against the soft knit cotton of her shirt, all uplifted into that stretch. Covey remembered that.

Covey began to save up images of this woman in her mind, to play them back to herself when she was alone.

Another image was the woman's hands cutting open boxes. The pocketknife with its worn handle fitting into her fist. The sudden deft motion—three slashes—and the blade snapping shut, and pocketed again.

Covey's favorite was the way the woman left at the end of the day. She rode a bicycle—a man's ten-speed. She'd wheel it into the street, one foot standing on the pedal and the other pushing off. Swerve in a lazy ellipse to change direction. Then lift her right leg straight back like a figure skater, across the bike. Lean down into the wind, pick up speed, and be gone.

It did not occur to Covey to approach this woman, to try to talk to her, or make herself known to her. She didn't even know if the woman had ever noticed her. She was content just to watch her, take her in, record these images of her in her mind. Let the woman become special to her—secretly—become hers.

One night, the woman from the place where she worked appeared in one of Covey's dreams. They were working together, side by side, marking prices on a box full of merchandise. Covey turned to smile at the woman, but the woman turned away from her. Then Covey asked, "What's wrong, Skye?" And the woman would not look at her, only said to the boxes she was marking, "My name is not Skye." Then Covey reached out to touch her, reaching out toward the fulfillment that, in dreams, could come from just touching, just reaching to touch. But suddenly the woman was gone.

That woke her, and she found herself still reaching, still straining toward that woman whose images she had collected and saved. Now she knew why she had. She had wanted them — wanted her — for nights like this one. And it was not enough. She could not bring it off — her fantasy — this woman was not Skye. This was a real woman, a woman she had no claim on. She could not fantasize things this woman might say to her, things this woman might like about her — did not even know if this woman *would* like her.

Fully awake now, she tried to conjure up Skye — Skye whom she had created to love, whom she *could* be sure of. Who had not, Covey realized, been with her for many days now. There was only the image of this other woman, a woman whose name she didn't even know. And yet next to her, Skye was no longer enough. It was not enough to love Skye, just to love a woman. She wanted to be *loved by* a woman, by a woman who could be much more than her own imagination could create.

In the morning, she did not look at anyone on the street, on the bus. She reached the place where she worked early, and found the woman who had been in her dream the night before, outside, locking her bike to the chain fence. Covey went over to her and said hello, and the woman looked up and smiled. "I work here, too," Covey told her.

The woman dropped her keys in her pocket and stood up. "I know. I've seen you around a lot. But I don't know what your name is."

"Covey. Kate Coverly. But everyone calls me Covey." She hesitated a few seconds as they both stared at each other in the bright morning sunlight, the short spell of silence hanging expectantly between them. Then she broke the spell. "What's your name?"

THE WOMAN WHO LOVED DANCING

The dance was a traditional women's dance, a Macedonian one called Žensko Krsteno. When the music ended, the long line of dancers broke apart into little clumps of individuals, waiting to hear what the next dance would be. Jessica kept holding my hand. She flashed me a conspiratorial smile, and pulled me over to an empty corner of the room.

"What is it?"

"Those two women over there—did you notice them? I think they're more than just close friends."

I followed the direction of her eyes. Two women I'd never seen before at our folkdance group were in the opposite corner of the room. One was brown-haired, and had on an embroidered peasant blouse; the other was wearing a navy blue T shirt, and she was blond. They were standing just a little bit closer to each other than necessary. And they did look enough like us to be suspect. I wouldn't have noticed, but Jess has a genius for noticing even the vaguest possibilities—probably a result of her having a few years more experience than me in this lifestyle.

"I hope they are." I studied them from the privacy created by the crowded room between us. "We could go introduce ourselves . . ." I broke off as another thought occurred, ". . . I hope they're folkdancers, I mean, that they'll keep coming here."

Jess nodded. "It'd be nice not to be the only gay couple for a change. Let's do lots of partner dances together and maybe they'll notice that we *are* a couple."

This was a convenient plan, since she and I always dance together, anyway. I always liked dancing with women, even before I converted. Long ago, I became convinced that women

are just better dancers—even women who think they can't
dance at all are hardly ever such disasters as some men who
think they can. Besides, being willing to dance with another
woman meant I always had a partner, while other women would
be sitting down because there weren't "enough men to go
around."

But I never really appreciated what couple dances were all
about until this past fall, when I first started to know Jessica,
and everything in my life began to be different. All of a sudden,
couple dances made sense—they were designed that way to
give me an excuse to watch her, touch her, follow her and lead
her—to flirt with her. Now, on the rare nights when there's a
"shortage of women," the men have learned not to interrupt
me and Jessica when we're dancing together. No, we wouldn't
rather be dancing with them.

"Do you want to do this?" Jessica was asking me. I realized
that the insipid schottische was finally over. The music playing
now was Dayagim.

When I dance with Jessica, every dance has its own special
places. In Dayagim, it's the part where she turns to come toward
me, just before we swing each other. I love the motion of that
change in direction, the way her hair streams out behind her,
and her eyes meet mine. Then all of her body is meeting me,
touching mine in that second's pause before we start to spin.
It's the same each time the music gets to that part, and I can't
take my eyes off of her.

That's the way it is whenever I dance with her. Almost whenever I'm with her, in fact. Even though it's months now, that
we've been seeing each other, we still seem to be centered in
that phase of the relationship where we could just stare into
each other's eyes for hours on end. . . . So we spend a lot of
time together, more every week that passes. My favorite of all
our time together is when we're dancing.

With Dayagim, the program started to pick up. Lesley, who
was running the records, put on a lot of the couple dances we
like: polses, zwiefachers, invertites. Even the dances she'd
chosen to teach, I wanted to learn. So I didn't get a break for
practically the whole evening.

Finally she played something that neither Jess nor I liked. We
dragged ourselves downstairs to the cold drink machine.

"Did you notice?" Jessica said, as soon as we were out of the room. "One of those women was dancing."

"Which one?"

"The one in the peasant blouse, obviously. She was right next to me for Seljančica. She's not bad, either. You can tell she's danced before by the way she does kolo steps."

"Maybe she's just been away from it for a long time," I suggested.

"I feel sorry for her."

"What?" That caught me completely off guard. For me, folkdancing is guaranteed satisfaction—one place I can count on having a good time. I wondered if I had heard right. "What are you talking about, Jessica?"

"I mean it. Because the other woman—the one who came with her—isn't a folkdancer."

It was true. As we came back upstairs, I could see that woman, the blond one, still standing in the same spot, near the door, with her hands shoved in her pockets, watching. Her friend, the brown-haired woman, was in the circle out on the dance floor. The other dance had ended, and now Lesley was teaching a kopanitsa. For a change, it was something Jess and I both knew, so we took our drinks to sit on one of the window seats.

I glanced back toward the woman near the door. "Maybe she'll decide it looks like fun, and she'll try it and end up being a folkdancer, too."

Jessica's look contradicted me. "That won't happen."

"How do you know?"

"I know." She said it with that air of certainty and finality she gets sometimes, that can make me wonder why I even asked such a question.

I shrugged. "Then maybe you should feel sorry for *her*. She's the one who's missing out."

Jessica shook her head. "I know what it's like for the one who's a dancer."

Something about Jessica's responses was making me curious. Most of the time, I feel as if I know her so well, I forget there is so much that we haven't had time to talk about, so much I don't know. I asked, "What's it like?"

"Well, she really loves folkdancing, and she used to come all the time before she met the other woman."

"I never saw her here."

"Not here." Her voice had a tinge of impatience. "It was somewhere else, some other dance group."

I realized she was telling me a story. I resolved not to interrupt again, leaned back against the shutters to listen.

"Maybe it was even in another city. Yeah. And it was years ago, so she's forgotten a whole lot of dances now. But she never forgot how much she loved them. She used to go folkdancing three or four nights a week. She bought records and practiced the steps at home in front of her mirror. She even got into studying folklore, and Balkan music, and the Serbo-Croatian language. She taught herself how to embroider and made pretty things for herself to dance in—aprons and kerchiefs and blouses. All of her friends were folkdancers. It was the interest her life centered around.

"Then she met the other woman. And she fell in love.

"The other woman didn't like folkdancing. The music didn't turn her on—she just couldn't feel the beat, if it was in 9/16's time. She thought the dances were "interesting"—to watch a few times a year. She thought the whole thing was a little much. The other woman was embarrassed by the costumes that the woman who loved dancing wore. She didn't like embroidery and fussiness. She liked clothes with clean lines, that were simple and crisp and definitive. The friends of the woman who loved dancing bored her. All they ever seemed to talk about was folkdancing. She liked to do other kinds of things, like going out to eat, and to movies, and to bars where women did the other kind of dancing. But she loved the woman who was a dancer. And they decided to move in together.

"Because she loved the other woman, the woman who loved dancing stopped folkdancing and began to go to bars and movies, too. But she didn't enjoy it. And after they'd been living together awhile, and the initial excitement had worn off, she wanted to dance again.

"She still loved the other woman just as much, and she'd ask her to come with her, to try it. But when the other woman went with her, she wouldn't try it—she'd stand in that corner and watch, and then she'd start making cutting remarks about the people. Later, she'd say that all folkdancers were straight, and that it wasn't her idea of a good time to hang out with a bunch of straight people all night. And it would usually end in a fight. "Then the woman who was a dancer would decide it would be better if she went alone. But the other woman couldn't help feeling jealous about her going out to have a good time without her. So when she came home, it would still end in a fight. Either way—that would be the result. There was no way to work it out...." Jessica fell silent.

Waiting for her to continue, I wondered. She hadn't been telling this like the stories she makes up sometimes, but as if it had actually happened. But how could she know so much about those two women? Was she talking about them at all, or someone else? I turned to look at her closely. She seemed to be way off lost somewhere, in her distance, her story.

Across the dance floor, the woman who loved dancing was still in the circle. They were up to the last sequence of steps and she was doing it perfectly. The other woman, the blond one, leaned against the wall, a wistful figure. She didn't look bitter or vindictive, just left out. I turned back to Jessica. "And then what?"

Her attention drawn back to me, she met my eyes, looked away. "That's all. We broke up."

The story was over. In a kind of wonder, I shuffled through its pieces in my mind, trying to pick out my feelings from the confusion it left me with. I turned to Jess. Her face was full of the hurtful memory. There seemed to be nothing I could say. What I wanted was to hold her, to be held by her. But we were in a public place. I put my hand on hers. She took it, squeezed it hard. "Maybe," I said, "the story will end happier this way."

The sounds of gajda and caval burst from the speakers. It was the music for the kopanitsa they'd been learning. Jessica shook off the reverie, jumping down from the window seat; I ran to follow her into the line.

In the dance, we were across the room from the woman with the brown hair. I kept watching her. It felt as if I knew her, or at least knew an intimate part of her life that she didn't know I knew. She had learned all the figures, was no longer even paying attention to the leader's feet. She saw me watching her and smiled across the circle. That disarmed me, made me think. I realized I didn't really know her at all. I wondered about her and her friend, what *their* story was. Her eyes were still on me, and I found myself returning her smile.

When the dance was over, Lesley began to lead Ličko Kolo. It is traditionally the last dance, and it's also traditional for everyone to dance, even people who've been sitting around all evening. The steps are very simple and slow—it's the music that's arresting, haunting. There is no record for this dance—it is sung by the dancers, just as women sang it to each other in the mountains of Yugoslavia years ago:

> Pjevaj mi pjevaj, sokole
> pjevaj mi pjevaj, sokole
> šalaj sokole. . . .

> Sing to me falcon
> as you sang last night
> under the window of my love
> My love lay asleep
> a cold stone beneath her head
> I took the stone away and
> replaced it
> with my arm.

Next to me, Jessica's voice dipped beneath mine into the rich harmony. Suddenly it seemed very special to have her there, next to me, in this ritual, very fortunate that all of this was something we could share.

As everyone held hands, I could feel the energy flow through the unbroken ring that slowly expanded to fill the whole dance floor. My eyes swept across the room. No one was left in the corners, around the edges of the wall, in the window seats, or by the door. I began to search the string of faces one by one, along the circle. Halfway around, I found what I was looking for. I squeezed Jessica's hand, nodded across the circle. Jess stared a few seconds, and then she saw her too—the other woman, the one who was not a dancer. She had taken her place in the circle next to the woman she loved.

WE USED TO BE BEST FRIENDS

"What makes you so sure it would work, anyway? Just that we're friends?"

Kelly nodded. "Just because we're friends. Because you're the best friend I've ever had."

Francie was stayed a moment by the sincerity in Kelly's gray eyes. That was one of the things she liked her for—that ability to come right out with feelings which others would have avoided mentioning or joked about. The way she and Kelly had always been able to say how they felt about each other. Right now, though, she felt a lot of reservations about Kelly's new idea.

"But what if it *didn't* work?" she said. "A lot of times, when friends live together, they get on each other's nerves. This way we can have fun when we get together. I don't want to spoil that. It's a whole different trip when you have to see somebody every day whether you want to or not—have to listen to music they want to hear, fix foods you don't even like, hang around with people you can't stand, just because those people are their friends—"

"Francie," Kelly interjected. "You're thinking about Alex. Not me." Francie stopped short. She *was* thinking about her former husband. "I wouldn't be like that," Kelly went on in a hurt voice. "Anyway, we already like the same foods and the same radio stations."

Francie was embarrassed, ashamed of comparing Kelly's friendship with the ugly fiasco that had been her marriage. She felt apologetic. "But where would we look for a place? We couldn't live around here—I don't think it would be safe for you—or me."

Kelly looked pensive and Francie knew that she, too, was thinking of the differences between them, differences most obvious in their looks—Kelly's white skin, straight gold hair, and her gray eyes behind the wire-rimmed glasses, in sharp contrast to Francie's chocolatey complexion and her fluffy dark afro. There were differences, too, in their backgrounds, like this neighborhood in the black community which had always been home to Francie, compared to Kelly's area only a few blocks south, but on the other side of the expressway, an area still almost totally white. And yet, Francie reflected, their interests and views were so similar that when they spent time together, the differences didn't matter. But sharing an apartment might be another story.

Francie giggled. "We certainly can't tell the landlady we're sisters, either."

Kelly laughed, then grew serious as she said, "But some parts of the city are integrated. Maybe we could live in the university section. The rents are higher, but if we shared a place we could afford more. I think we could find a place if we both really wanted to."

It was true. Francie tried to be truthful, too. "If I ever *was* going to stop living alone, I'd want to live with you. But I like this place. It's the only place I've ever lived that's all mine. And it feels like it's only since I've been living here that I've started to find out what I *do* like, how I want to live, what I'm like. I don't know if I could give that up—yet."

After Kelly had gone, Francie continued to think about living with her. She knew it was appealing. Ever since they had become friends, Kelly had been special to her in a way no other friend had ever approached. It would be fun to decorate an apartment together, to cook meals for each other, kind of look after one another. Yet it scared her to think of living with, of depending on anyone—even Kelly.

She wandered into the other room, thinking how much she loved this small apartment, this tiny bedroom with its quaint slanted ceilings and plain wood floors. She loved most the way in which it was hers—curtains she had made hanging in the dormer windows, her favorite books lined up on the shelf, the little patchwork quilt her grandmother had given her when Francie was twelve, that covered the single bed. Everything mirrored her, affirmed her sense of self, and could reassure her when she felt depressed, frightened, or insecure. Or lonely, as she often did after Kelly left.

Her eye was caught by a framed photograph of a small black girl with her hair braided in two shiny pigtails, who smiled out into Francie's eyes—a little girl with the same round face, snub nose, and square chin as Francie's—Jeanice. Instantly, Francie's thoughts flashed back through the past five years—the marriage that had resembled a badly plotted soap opera, the husband who turned out not to be the admirable young hero after all, the baby she couldn't care for properly after returning to work, the withdrawal in defeat to her mother's. Perhaps she had never fully recovered. Though she had put her own life back together, saved money and rented this apartment, she had never been able to completely shake her sense of failure. And Jeanice had lived at her mother's ever since.

Francie picked up the picture and gazed into those deep brown eyes. What had she been thinking of? If she was ever going to live with another person again, that person must be her daughter. Jeanice had asked many times when her mother would live with her again, had always been put off with vague answers about some day. Francie *did* want to live with Jeanice again. But she still felt there was so much more she needed to have together in her own life before she could be the kind of mother she wanted to be for Jeanice.

Francie listened intently as the unanswered phone at the other end of the line kept ringing. Over the sound came the sudden raucous buzzing of her own doorbell. She dropped the receiver back on the hook and ran to answer the door. It was Kelly.

"I've just been trying to call you, Kell. Where *were* you?"

Kelly looked guiltily at her watch. "I guess I *am* late. I'm sorry. You're not angry are you?"

"No, just glad you're here. But the meat loaf is probably furious." Francie found she seldom grew angry over such things. The unpredictableness—not being on time, or showing up an hour early or on a day they had not planned to get together at all—was part of Kelly's nature. Always, Francie just felt happy to see her.

As they began eating dinner, Francie found herself only half listening to Kelly's stream of talk, engrossed in watching Kelly—face still flushed and rosy from the early October cold, eyes sparkling as she talked, hands alternating between accentuating her words and devouring her meal. All of it was so typically Kelly—no one else could talk so much and eat so much at the same time.

"I didn't tell you yet why I was late," Kelly said. "You know that meeting I told you I was going to, for the new women's center?"

"Oh, yeah." Francie remembered now, Kelly's telling her about the plans for the center, and asking her last week if she wanted to go to the meeting.

"Well," Kelly went on, "maybe you were smart not to want to spend Saturday afternoon cooped up in a meeting. It went on forever and ever and ever. But afterwards, I got to talking with some of the other women. And this one woman who was really nice told me some of them were going out to dinner together. She invited me to come along, but I wouldn't have passed up one of your meals for the best restaurant in the city—which of course they weren't planning to go to anyhow. So then she told me about this bar where they were going afterwards, and I thought you might like to go there and meet some of them."

"A bar?" Francie was surprised. Kelly knew that she didn't especially like bars or night clubs. Kelly had never seemed interested in that kind of thing, either.

"Well, it sounded different. Not like you're thinking. For one thing, she said it's mostly women who go there—only a few men. And that it's quiet—they play tapes, and sometimes they have entertainment, like folksingers. She said they serve food, too, so people don't go in there just to get drunk."

"Where is it? What's it called?"

"It's called Judy's," Kelly said. "It's at Fifth and University."

Sometimes, Francie did not know why she went along with Kelly's crazy ideas. Kelly would suggest things so improbable —like going to the zoo in the middle of winter, or going horseback riding when neither had ever been on a horse in her life. And Francie would find herself doing them, and actually enjoying it, picking up the sense of mischievousness from Kelly. Kelly was drawing her on with that impish grin right now. "Come on,

Francie,'' she said. "It's Saturday night. We'll do the town."
And Francie found herself grinning back and saying o.k.

The place was inconspicuous—no neon signs announcing its
name, no crowd of drunks outside, no loud music blaring forth
as they pulled open the door. They made their way to the bar
and ordered drinks, then found a table and sat down, since the
women from the meeting had apparently not yet arrived. As
Francie's eyes adjusted to the smoky darkness, she began to
look around. Though a few men were scattered here and there,
most of the people, as Kelly had predicted, were women—
women of different ages and sizes and colors. Most were white,
but some were black, and a handful looked Asian or Hispanic.
They were talking quietly over the soft music, and at the back
of the room, Francie could just discern a number of couples on
the shadowy dance floor.

"Well, what do you think?" Kelly asked.

"It seems all right." Francie tasted her drink.

"I like it," Kelly said. "I'm finding more and more that I like
going to places where I can be with women."

Francie nodded agreement. "Every other time I've gone to a
bar, I felt like I was on the defensive the whole time—keeping
watch on all the unattached men and preparing how to get rid
of them when they finally got around to approaching me."

Kelly laughed. "That doesn't seem to be a problem here."

As she sipped her drink, Francie began to study the people
around her. She and Kelly often liked to watch people in crowds
and pick out those who looked interesting, like the type they
might want to become friends with. It was fun to see if they
chose the same ones. "That woman over there—" Francie
nodded, "with the corduroy jeans and the real short afro. She
looks like she might be a poet or a playwright or something."
While Francie watched, the woman carried two drinks over to
another woman, a white woman, and casually put her arm
around the other's shoulders. Francie glanced back to smile at
Kelly, but Kelly seemed to have missed it, was busy stirring the
remains of her drink.

Francie finished hers, and got up to make her way to the
ladies' room at the back of the dance floor. When she reached
the end of the tables she stopped, her attention caught by the
couples slow-dancing with their arms around each other. It

registered with a shock. They were all women. And even as she stood there, a woman came up to her and asked, "Want to dance?"

Francie turned and fled back to the table, forgetting completely why she had gotten up in the first place. "Kelly, let's go. Let's get out of here." Kelly looked up in surprise, but responded immediately to the alarm in Francie's eyes and voice. She pulled on her jacket and they left.

Francie didn't say anything more until they were in the car and Kelly had started the motor. Then, as they pulled into traffic, she burst out, "Those women! They were all lesbians!"

Kelly didn't take her eyes off the road. "Yeah? What about it?" Though the words were light, casual, Kelly's voice sounded odd—strained and tense—and Francie turned to look at her suspiciously.

"Kelly, did you know that? Did you know it would be all lesbians?"

Kelly's voice still sounded strange. "I didn't really know," she said slowly, "But I thought it might be. And I thought, if it was, it would be kind of fun. After all, you've always liked to do things that were—new and different, before."

"But a bar for lesbians? That's not the same. Kelly, those women in there must have thought you and I were—just like them."

"Maybe we're not so different," Kelly said.

But Francie hardly heard her. "Why didn't you tell me, Kelly? Why didn't you tell me before we went there?"

Kelly's voice was very small. "I thought you wouldn't come with me."

"But why did you want to go there anyway? Why would you want to be around all those misfits?"

Kelly didn't answer. She stared through the windshield, her lips tightly compressed. And the silence that settled between them grew more intense with each passing block. Francie felt shivers run through her despite the warmth from the car heater and her heavy coat. She hugged her arms closer around her and waited. But Kelly still had not broken the silence as they pulled up before Francie's building. Finally Francie said, "Come on, Kelly. What's the matter?"

Kelly snapped bitterly, "You wouldn't understand."

The sharp words stung like a slap in Francie's face. She stared at Kelly in amazement for a second, then quickly collected her purse and scarf, got out of the car, and slammed the door behind her.

The quarrel caused a rent in the friendship that grew as the days went by. Kelly didn't call, and Francie did not try to call Kelly. She still felt too confused—and too hurt. As she often did when she was troubled, she began to go frequently to her mother's, and to spend a lot of time with Jeanice. She loved to see Jeanice's face light up when she arrived, loved holding her on her lap while they read stories, or tucking her into bed at night. Yet, often when she was with Jeanice she felt guilty. Guilty that she wasn't more of a mother. Guilty, too, because much as she enjoyed being with her, she knew she was using Jeanice as an escape—an escape from her apartment, which suddenly seemed empty, from the long eventless evenings and weekends which stretched out before her, from the absence of something, someone enormously important in her life—Kelly.

She had quarrelled with friends before—broken off with them. It had never hurt like this. She'd forgotten those others but she couldn't forget Kelly, found herself wishing on the few occasions when the doorbell or phone rang that it would be Kelly—and so disappointed when it was not that she felt like crying. Still, she could not bring herself to make the first move toward reconciliation.

It was nearly three weeks later when Francie stopped at her favorite bookstore on her way from work. She was browsing in the fiction section when she felt someone's eyes on her. She turned abruptly, and her eyes met Kelly's.

Francie was surprised at her own reaction. She had thought she would still feel resentment for the hurt Kelly had caused her. And yet, when she looked at Kelly standing there in that familiar pose, with her hands in the pockets of her pea coat and that crazy six-foot purple scarf around her neck, Francie felt exactly as she always did when Kelly appeared anywhere —just glad to see her. In spite of herself, the corners of Francie's mouth turned up in a smile. "Kelly!"

Kelly's face relaxed with relief. "Francie. I was afraid you weren't going to speak to me. Then you're not still pissed off?"

Francie wanted to forgive Kelly immediately, but she knew it was not that simple. "Are you?" she asked.

"No," Kelly answered. Then she looked at the floor. "But I do want to talk to you, to try to—explain something to you." She looked up again. "Are you busy tonight?"

"No—well, I promised my mother I'd drop off some stuff for her church rummage sale. But I don't have to stay—it wouldn't take me long."

"Then maybe you could come over to my place, after you do that?"

Francie nodded. "Would around 7:30 be o.k.?"

"Sure. I'll be home all evening."

Francie sat in the car outside Kelly's building trying to pull her thoughts together before she went in. She remembered how hurt and betrayed she had felt the night they had quarrelled. She was ready for that to be over. And she felt a growing excitement, knowing that it *would* be over soon, that she and Kelly could go on being friends again. It ought to be easy. But it didn't feel easy to get out of the car and walk into the vestibule. She could hear her heart beating as Kelly buzzed her into the building, feel her legs shaking as she climbed the three flights of stairs to Kelly's door.

Kelly put on a kettle for coffee, and they sat in the kitchen waiting for the water to boil. Francie's eyes travelled over the familiar assortment of cookbooks, canisters, potholders, spices. Everything was the same as always—except Kelly. Usually she was so animated—constantly moving, talking, laughing. Tonight she poured the coffee, added the cream and sugar without a word. They faced each other across the little table. The refrigerator's hum and the hissing radiator were suddenly loud as the two women each stirred the coffee.

"I feel really bad about the other night," Kelly said, breaking the stillness. "I didn't mean to. . . hurt you."

Francie watched the steam curl upward from her cup. "I guess what hurt me was that you wouldn't talk to me. I didn't understand what was going on."

"Well," Kelly said slowly, "it felt like you were attacking me personally. Putting me down."

Francie shook her head. "I wasn't trying to put you down. I

just didn't understand why you would want to go to a bar like that, a place for lesbians."

"I guess I was curious about it. I wanted to see what it would be like." Kelly looked up to meet Francie's eyes. "Didn't you ever wonder about lesbians?"

"What are you trying to get at, Kelly?"

"Well, didn't you? Didn't you ever wonder what it would be like to be a lesbian? Wasn't there ever a time in your life when you were attracted to another woman, or a girl, maybe in high school?"

"Oh, in high school. Yeah—I had a crush on my French teacher when I was in ninth grade. And there was a girl in my class that I thought was really neat. I even tried to dress like her and talk like her and I kept wishing she would notice me, if that's what you mean. But what has that got to do with anything?"

Kelly's face was serious, intent. "Yeah, that's sort of what I mean. Only more than that. I mean somebody you wanted to be with all the time and wanted to love, even more than you could as a friend. . . ." She looked away. Drew her knees up close to her on the kitchen chair, hugged her arms around them, took off her glasses to rest her head on her knees, looking off across the kitchen as she went on.

"I have a friend," she said softly, "that I feel that way about. We were best friends. But it's started to feel different—for me, anyway. Like she's more than just my friend. I feel like I want to be with her all the time, and I can't stop thinking about her, even when I'm not with her. When I know I'm going to see her, I look forward to it all day. I feel excited whenever I do see her, and when I look at her I just keep thinking how pretty she is and I want to touch her. I can't help it—I'm in love with her. I've been trying to find ways to tell her how I feel, but I just can't seem to do it right. I guess I'm afraid she'll reject me and I couldn't bear to lose her as a friend. She might feel the same way about me, but I don't know. . . ." Kelly's voice stopped, her last words hanging like a question.

Francie could not think what to say. She had to answer something, anything. Perhaps she hadn't understood right. Perhaps Kelly didn't really mean what Francie thought. Yet the words that came out sounded unnecessary even to herself. "Who is she?"

And Kelly answered, "You know who she is."

Francie got up with a clumsy scrape of the chair. She felt the need to move and crossed the room to the window, stared out a long minute at the blank wall of the building next door. When she turned back to the table, she realized that Kelly was crying. Silent tears filled her eyes and ran down her face. Automatically, Francie moved toward Kelly with the urge to embrace her, to hold and comfort her. Within inches of Kelly's gold head, she stopped, her arms still upraised. If she did that now, what would Kelly think? She hesitated a moment, her arms falling awkwardly to her sides. "I...I don't know what to say," she stammered. "I think I understand what you're trying to tell me but...I don't know how to answer."

Kelly still would not look at her, but she said, "You don't have to be polite. If you're turned off or you...hate me, you might as well tell me now."

"No, Kelly, I don't hate you. It's just something I never thought about before. I didn't know you were...feeling like that. And I'm not sure yet how I feel about it. I guess I should probably go home. I'd like to be by myself and think about this for awhile— before we talk about it any more."

Kelly, still hunched up on the chair, was silent. Francie repeated, "Just give me some time to think, o.k.?" But the words felt small, inadequate. She reached out a hand and saw her own fingers shaking. Gently, she touched Kelly's shoulder. "O.k., Kelly?" she asked again.

"O.k."

Francie hardly slept all that night, and went through the motions of the next day in a daze. Her mind was always on Kelly, what Kelly had told her, what Kelly was asking her. She forced herself to examine her own feelings about Kelly, to explore how strong they were. She thought of how it always felt so exciting and special to see Kelly. Was it possible that she was attracted to Kelly? She had to admit to herself how much she liked to look at her, how good it felt when they touched or hugged each other, how much it meant to her when Kelly told her things she liked about her. She had to admit, too, how devastated she had been by their quarrel, how much she had missed Kelly the past few weeks, how much she already wanted to see her again, even now. Were her own feelings really so different from Kelly's? Could she call it love? Could she deny that it was?

When she left work that evening, Francie went again to the bookstore. She ignored the novels that usually drew her, and began to search through the non-fiction. Finally, in a section she had never explored, she found what seemed to be what she wanted—a book called *When Women Love Each Other.* There were other books with similar titles on the same shelf. Her face was burning and she was sure every eye in the store was upon her, but she picked out two more paperbacks and carried them to the counter. She tried to convince herself that she bought them out of concern for Kelly, for any subject so important to a friend as close as Kelly. But she knew, as she brought the books home, and later, as she stayed up reading until the early hours of morning, that it was really herself she was searching for in the descriptions on these pages.

In a strange way, the books were comforting, reassuring. But even they could not give her an answer for Kelly. And when she asked herself, no words came—only the image of Kelly left huddled on that kitchen chair, crying.

The following night, Francie went to her mother's. She walked slowly, through streets she had played in as a child, past the corner grocer's, the church where she had spent so many Sunday mornings, houses of neighbors. Wondered what they would think if they knew what she had been contemplating for the past couple of days. She was already considered stand-offish and uppity in this community—because she no longer attended church, because she wouldn't go out with any of the men, because she was so friendly with whites. But what kind of an outcast would it make her if she continued this friendship in the direction Kelly wanted it to go?

She approached the small brick row house, wondering what her mother would think if she knew what was going on in Francie's mind. Of course, Francie had no intention of actually telling her, but she might be able to feel her out a little. And just her mother's presence would be some support. Francie had purposely waited until after Jeanice's bedtime, in order to be alone with her mother.

As she ascended the porch steps, she could hear angry voices from inside—first her mother's voice, then the voice of Francie's youngest brother, Kenny, shouting in return. Before Francie could turn the knob, the door was flung back and Kenny stormed out, pushed past her, and took off down the street. Francie rushed into the living room. "What's going on?" she asked her mother breathlessly.

"That boy will be the death of me. I know he doesn't like it, but he's just going to have to get used to it." Her mother sighed. "Take off your coat, Francie. Come on in the kitchen." Francie dumped her coat on the couch and followed her mother back to the kitchen where her mother sank heavily into a chair. "I've been meaning to tell you this, Francie, but it seemed like you always had so many other things on your mind I just kept putting it off. I've decided to move back to South Carolina."

"What?"

"You heard me right. This city's just no place any more to be trying to raise a teenage boy. You know the way the kids are nowadays—the gangs. If Kenny keeps on going along with those friends of his, he's liable to end up in real bad trouble. And if he doesn't, they'll be after him."

Francie could only respond, "But South Carolina?"

"Lancaster County. Where your Aunt Irene lives."

"That's the country!"

"That's right," her mother said. "And it's a nice place, too. You were born there, you know."

Francie's mind filled up with objections. "But you always said you were never going back there. You and Dad always said it was no place to raise kids. That everything was better up north —the jobs, the housing, the schools. . . ."

"I know," her mother said wistfully. "I used to believe it, too. But times have changed, Francie. It seems like there's just as much hate and discrimination here as there ever was down south. The schools aren't even integrated any more, and they've got cops in the halls all the time now, the kids are so bad. Since your father died it's not so easy, trying to do things by myself. It'll be good to be around my family again. Irene's oldest boy— you remember your cousin, Michael—he's the same age as Kenny. And Linda's just a year older than Jeanice, so she'll have a playmate, too."

"Jeanice!" Suddenly the full impact of what her mother was saying hit Francie. "You're going to take Jeanice?"

Her mother looked at her closely. "I was planning to. Unless, of course, you want to take her to stay with you."

Francie opened her mouth but no words came. Always, in the back of her mind had been the thought that some day she would have Jeanice with her. Some day when she had a better job, when she could afford a bigger apartment, when.... "When are you thinking of leaving?" she asked.

"Next summer. Soon as school lets out." Her mother looked at her hopefully. "Maybe you'd like to come with us, Francie. I know it's been hard for you, too. You might meet somebody nice down there and start out all over again. You never know."

Francie shook her head. She didn't want to meet any more men. She didn't want to move to South Carolina and leave— Kelly. Kelly, again. Why was she thinking of Kelly when she should be thinking of Jeanice?

"You don't have to make up your mind right away," her mother was saying. "There's still a good seven months till June. Even after that—you know you'd be welcome to come down any time, either to stay or to pick up Jeanice—whenever you get it together."

The words caught like a barb in Francie's mind. What was it, anyway, that she never felt she had "together"? Was it really her concerns about a bigger apartment and more money, or were they just excuses? She could not define what she really wanted—only to come to some kind of terms with herself, to grow clear of the tangled confusion she still felt about who she was, what really mattered in her life—confusion that was worse than ever as she thought now of Jeanice, now of Kelly. Her mother had stopped talking and was, Francie realized, waiting for some answer. "I...I don't know, Mom. I have to think about all this. I'll have to let you know."

Before she saw Kelly again, Francie had meant to arrive at some sort of answer. But now that a new problem faced her, she felt urgently the need to talk to her friend, and called to ask her over. As she opened the door, Francie noticed immediately that Kelly's face was drawn and looked as if she, too, had not been sleeping. Francie felt a wave of compassion, felt bad planning to dump still another problem in Kelly's lap. But before she could reconsider, Kelly asked, "What's on your mind?" And

Francie, in a rush, spilled out the story.

When it was finished, Kelly said thoughtfully, "I've always wondered how you felt about Jeanice. You hardly ever talk about her. It seemed like you'd kind of given up on being her mother."

"Given up? How could I give that up? I'll always be her mother, whether she lives with me or not. And anyway, I've always thought she *would* live with me some day. She's more important to me than—just about anyone else in the world."

"Then you're going to take her?"

"Oh, Kell, I don't know. I want to, but I don't see how I can do it, all by myself."

"You don't have to do it all by yourself," Kelly said.

"Who else am I going to depend on?"

Kelly started to reply, then stopped. Instead, she answered slowly, "At one of those meetings I've been going to—for the women's center—we were talking about children. Some of those women are alone, too, and have kids. They were talking about working out babysitting together, trying to depend on each other. And some of them have their kids in day care centers—one woman who said she does is a nurse's aide, so she can't make any more money than you."

Francie nodded. "It's not just the money," she conceded. "It's me. I just feel like I'm not ready yet. And I'm really scared, sometimes, that I'll never be ready."

Kelly was frowning in thought. "What is it you feel like you need, before you'll be ready?"

Francie was aware of a long time passing before she could answer, and when she did, it was over a lump in her throat. "I need to like myself more. I don't want to feel guilty anymore, or like I'm not good enough. And I want—maybe this sounds clichéd and idealistic—but I just want to be happier."

"What would make you happier?"

Francie shook her head. "I'm not sure I know."

"Maybe," Kelly was looking at her own hands, twisting a ring round and round on her finger, "maybe you'd be happier if you'd let someone love you."

When she finally answered, Francie's voice was barely more than a whisper. "Maybe you're right."

"And maybe," Kelly went on, "if you felt better about your-

self, you might be able to love Jeanice even more—enough to let
her live with you."

"You really think I *should* have her living with me, don't you?"

"Francie," Kelly's face was earnest, troubled, "I can't tell you
what to do. It's not fair for me to try to convince you one way or
the other. If you really want to be with her, you should. And you
know I'd help you any way I could. But if you don't..." she
shrugged. "You've got to do whatever you feel like you need to
do, for yourself."

"But just tell me this," Francie pressed. "What would you
do if you had a little girl?"

"If I had a little girl," Kelly said, looking straight into Francie's
eyes, "and I really loved her and cared about her, and she loved
me—I'd want to be with her. I'd do anything I could to be with
her, to live with her. I'd try to let her know all the time, how
much I loved her. And I'd try to make her happy."

And Francie knew suddenly that they were no longer talking
about Jeanice. "Kelly," she asked softly, "is that what you want?"

"I want you to let me love you. And I want...well...maybe
you'd feel like you could love me, too."

And Francie found herself saying the words it had taken her
so long to realize. "I do love you, Kelly. I never knew it before,
but I love you." Then, as the impact of her own words was reflected in Kelly's face, she added, "It's only that I never thought
I would be...or could be...a lesbian." Abruptly she burst into
tears. She covered her face with her hands, then buried her
head in her arms on the table, shaking with sobs.

Through her tears, she heard Kelly's voice. "I know, Francie.
I know—it's scary, it's heavy. But it isn't bad. It isn't wrong. I
know it's not—not what I feel, what you feel. We can have something together that's really beautiful. And whatever you decide
to do about Jeanice—or anything else—I'll try to support you."

Francie heard the words, wanted to believe them, but she
could not stop crying. She felt Kelly's hands, tentative at first,
on her hair, her shoulders. How long it had been since they had
touched each other, hugged each other as they used to do. Yet
Kelly's touch felt different now, full of a warmth and tenderness that made Francie yearn for more, to be even closer. Still
crying, she lifted her head, turned, and let Kelly take her in
her arms.

WHERE THE JOURNEY BEGAN

If I had asked her, Sierra probably could have told me I'd return. She can tell things like that—tell when it's going to rain, or tell which flowers will come up again in the same place next spring. She can tell a lot about me.

Sometimes she knows things about me before I know them. Like knowing when I'm about to get depressed. Or, if I were already feeling bad, she would know what it was that had happened. She knew long before I did that I was falling in love with her. Sierra knew, too, that I'd go away. She was telling me it was all right if I had to go, while I was still insisting that everything was fine, I was happy, I would stay with her. I was wrong.

I used to not like it, the way she knew so much about me. Knew even more than the usual details people around here seem to know about the business of everyone in the county. I used to feel exposed—embarrassed. Now it's different. I want there to be somebody else, one other person who knows me as I know myself now.

Where I've just come from, no one knew anyone. They'd pass each other in the street and not speak. I used to see the same people every morning, going away from home, every evening, going back home. They never greeted me. They never greeted each other. People lived in the same building and did not know each other's names. Everyone lived behind locked doors. I don't want to live like that. I don't care if Sierra knows everything about me, guesses my thoughts, laughs at my mistakes, my past. I don't mind so much what others know either.

A lot of things are different, now that I'm coming back. I left in the spring, early, when the branches were bare so that, from

where I am now, about halfway up the hill, you could see clear
back to the highway, to the river. Now the maples are in flame,
and there's nothing but a counterpane of color down the valley.
The roadside's full of milkweed and white snakeroot, which I
love the smell of. I've seen fall here before, but what's different
is the way it makes me feel—like crying. I have to keep stopping,
to bend down and touch things with my fingers, to pick up a
yellow leaf, or smell the pungent white blossoms. Swallow the
lump in my throat.

I'm different—just taking the time to savor this. I used to be
always in a rush, impatient; there were too many things I wanted
to do. Now it's taking me all afternoon to climb the five miles
up Acorn Hill Road to Sierra's cabin.

I used to be so restless. Always wanting things to change. And
Sierra stayed the same. She followed the same patterns day
after day—I'd watch her: First thing in the morning she'd go
out to the garden. Every morning, even in winter, even in the
snow. At the end of the day she'd watch the sunset. Sometimes,
last spring, I used to go with her, up to the ridge of Acorn Hill
where you can see for miles. We wouldn't talk to each other.
Just sit still and watch it, the way the people I've left watched
their television sets.

Watching the sunset or anything else, Sierra could be still
for hours. Once she sat on the porch and watched a spider spin
a whole web from one railing to the other. And she never swept
it down. Sometimes she went to the garden before the sun came
up. She said she liked to watch the flowers open on the zucchini
vines.

I could never be still that way. I couldn't stay put. Sierra tried.
She gave me packets of seeds to plant—onions, carrots, things
that took a long time. She thought it would help me to slow down,
waiting for them to grow. I seeded the garden, but I left before
the summer had even begun. Still she tried. Sierra was making
a quilt for me. Patchwork. The name of it was Blazing Star.
Tiny, tiny pieces that must all be sewn together. Even with me
helping, it would take months to finish. She wanted me to stay.

Part of me wanted to stay, stay with Sierra, anyway. It wasn't
her I wanted to leave. It was the sameness, the stillness, the
predictability. The way nothing ever changed—even the way
she never changed. I couldn't tell her that, though I think she

knew. When she realized I was set on leaving, and she asked me why, I tried to make light of it. Teased her that I was off to seek my fortune. Told her I wanted to find a name. I didn't have a name then, not an honest, taken, country name like Sierra.

Sierra is like the name she chose—strong, intense, and ruggedly beautiful. Sometimes catching her eyes is like finding wild violets in the woods where you least expect them. Her clothes are faded to the colors of earth. Her brown hair in two long braids is streaked with iron grey like veins of metal through stone. Enduring.

I was just the opposite—could never stick with anything. I'd pick half a gallon of berries and then forget to make the pie. Bring home a load of manure and leave it sitting in the truck all week. I was always making plans—to build a greenhouse, raise bees, build a windmill. Maybe I can do those things now, one at a time. Maybe Sierra still has the instructions I sent away for, the ones for those and half a dozen other projects. I was just some kind of hummingbird. A dragonfly. That's what she used to call me, name she gave me—Dragonfly. I have my own name now.

The higher I climb, the more the wind picks up, full of the scent of fall—ripe apples on the ground below an old tree I pass. Last year, Sierra and I gathered bushels to take to the cider press. It looks as if she hasn't been here this fall. On the wind, there's woodsmoke from some other cabin, maybe Ginger and Cedar's across the way. We'll have a fire tonight, too—if everything is still the same. It's growing cold enough already, the trees casting long shadows across the road. I'd pull another sweater out of my pack, but I'm almost there.

Already at the garden. It's dense and green and it suddenly seems a miracle that this could be here, inside the same fence where there was only bare earth when I left last spring. It's just squash, pumpkins, peppers, tomatoes—the same as any fall, but I can't go past without stopping, squatting. There's still a lot of food to put up for this winter. I remember how to do that. In the corner, where I planted the seeds she gave me, the onions are long and green, the carrot tops full and bushy.

The sun is behind the hill. It's quiet around the house. Sierra will be up the hill, watching the end of the sunset. Acorns are all over the yard, in front of the house. That's the biggest oak

around, Sierra's favorite tree. She used to call it her friend.
She'd speak to it when she went into or out of the house, and
I've seen her go up and put her arms around it, throw back her
head to whisper up into the leaves. Where I've been, they would
laugh at someone who did that. They would send them away. I
cross the yard to say hello to the oak, put my cheek against the
bark, wonder if it missed me.

At the steps, I take off my heavy pack and let it down on the
porch. The door is not locked. It never is. But I can't go into the
house—I don't know if I belong here. I sit on the porch to wait.
I don't mind now, waiting, sitting so still doing nothing except
smelling the clematis vine that's blooming late this year, all over
the railing, nothing except watching the sky go dark at one side
and red at the other. So still that I hear her coming down the
path from Acorn Hill—the leaves crunching under her feet,
and a mournful tune she's whistling—long before I see her. I
strain to listen, but can't tell yet—though one of the women
from the valley farm, who gave me a ride to the foot of this hill,
told me I'd find everything the same at Sierra's place. I can't
tell for sure until I see her come into the clearing—yes, she's
alone.

I'd expected it to be quiet, my return. Could picture walking
into the cabin and Sierra looking up from her quilting frame as
if I'd only been gone picking blackberries for the afternoon,
smiling quietly as I re-entered her life. Not all this commotion—
the way she's running, her braids flying, shouting at me across
the clearing—"You're home!" Laughing so much that I am, too,
when she throws her arms around me.

She's still laughing, teasing me, asking, "Have you found your
fortune yet?"

I think I have.

"Dragonfly—" she says, and stops, and asks me if I've found
a name.

I tell her. My name is Sojourner.

She lets go of me to search my face. "For where you're going?"

"No, for where I've been."

"Then you'll stay?" How can she doubt it? Sierra who always
knew what would happen, who was always sure of everything
in her life? And does it make such a difference to her?

The tears have collected again in my throat so that I can't

answer. She takes me by the hand and draws me into the house, and we stand in the doorway, hand in hand, while I look again at the one room that is all of this house. On the wall, the shelves are filling up with glass—fruit and vegetables, pickles and preserves put up for the winter, jars of seeds, dried fruit and grain. Bunches of mint, of chamomile hang upside-down in the darkening window, braids of onions on the wall.

She's right. I'm home.

"Sierra, it's all the same," I finally say. "Everything has stayed the same."

She says no. "Nothing is the same. Nothing has been the same since you went away."

She strikes a match to light a lantern against the twilight. The crate for wood by the stove is nearly empty; I'll bring in more for the morning. I can see the ladder to the loft where we'll sleep tonight. Every inch of space is in use.

This little house will be our gypsy wagon. Full, intense, rich, it is like her.

Across the room, there's a quilt stretched on the frame, ready for finishing—pieced from one thousand tiny diamonds, a thousand colors. One immense, blazing star.